PENGUIN CLASSICS

GUNNAR'S DAUGHTER

Sigrid Undset (1882–1949) was born in Denmark, the eldest daughter of a Norwegian father and a Danish mother, and moved with her family to Oslo two years later. She published her first novel, *Fru Marta Oulie* (*Mrs. Marta Oulie*) in 1907 and her second, *Den lykkelige alder* (*The Happy Age*), in 1908. The following year she published her first work set in the Middle Ages, *Fortællingen om Viga-Ljot og Vigdis* (later translated into English under the title *Gunnar's Daughter*). More novels and stories followed, including *Jenny* (1911, translated 1920), *Fattige skjaebner* (*Fates of the Poor*, 1912), *Vaaren* (*Spring*, 1914), *Splinten av troldspeilet* (translated in part as *Images in a Mirror*, 1917), and *De kloge jomfruer* (*The Wise Virgins*, 1918). Most of these early works have never been translated into English. In 1920 Undset published the first volume of *Kristin Lavransdatter*, the medieval trilogy that would become her most famous work. *Kransen* (*The Wreath*) was followed by *Husfrue* (*The Wife*) in 1921 and *Korset* (*The Cross*) in 1922. Beginning in 1925 she published the four-volume *Olav Audunssøn i Hestviken* (translated into English under the title *The Master of Hestviken*), also set in the Middle Ages. In 1928 Sigrid Undset won the Nobel Prize for Literature. During the 1930s she published several more novels, notably the autobiographical *Elleve aar* (translated as *The Longest Years*, 1934). She was also a prolific essayist on subjects ranging from Scandinavian history and literature to the Catholic church (to which she became a convert in 1924) and politics. During the Nazi occupation of Norway, Undset lived as a refugee in New York City. She returned home in 1945 and lived in Lillehammer until her death in 1949.

Sherrill Harbison is a Visiting Lecturer at Trinity College, Hartford, and an Associate of the Five Colleges (Amherst, Smith, Mount Holyoke, Hampshire, and the University of Massachusetts). She received her B.A. in Art History from Oberlin College and her Ph.D. in English from the University of Massachusetts at Amherst, where she also taught for five years. Her work on Sigrid Undset has been supported by the Fulbright Association and the Norwegian Marshall Fund, and she has won three times the Aurora Borealis Prize, awarded by the Five Nordic Governments to an American scholar. She has published articles on Undset, Willa Cather, and William Faulkner, and has translated some of Undset's shorter works.

T0200834

GUNNAR'S DAUGHTER

SIGRID UNDSET

Translated by Arthur G. Chater
EDITED WITH AN INTRODUCTION
AND NOTES BY SHERRILL HARBISON

PENGUIN BOOKS

PENGUIN BOOKS

Published by the Penguin Group

Penguin Group (USA) Inc., 375 Hudson Street, New York, New York 10014, U S.A

Penguin Group (Canada), 90 Eglinton Avenue East, Suite 700, Toronto,
Ontario, Canada M4P 2Y3 (a division of Pearson Penguin Canada Inc)

Penguin Books Ltd, 80 Strand, London WC2R 0RL, England

Penguin Ireland, 25 St Stephen's Green, Dublin 2, Ireland (a division of Penguin Books Ltd)

Penguin Group (Australia), 250 Camberwell Road, Camberwell,
Victoria 3124, Australia (a division of Pearson Australia Group Pty Ltd)

Penguin Books India Pvt Ltd, 11 Community Centre, Panchsheel Park, New Delhi – 110 017, India

Penguin Group (NZ), cnr Airborne and Rosedale Roads,
Albany, Auckland 1310, New Zealand (a division of Pearson New Zealand Ltd)

Penguin Books (South Africa) (Pty) Ltd, 24 Sturdee Avenue,
Rosebank, Johannesburg 2196, South Africa

Penguin Books Ltd, Registered Offices· 80 Strand, London WC2R 0RL, England

First published in the United States of America
by Alfred A Knopf, Inc 1936
Published by arrangement with Alfred A. Knopf, Inc.
This edition with an introduction and notes by
Sherrill Harbison published in Penguin Books 1998

15 17 19 20 18 16 14

Translation copyright Alfred A. Knopf, Inc., 1936
Copyright © renewed Alfred A. Knopf, Inc., 1964
Introduction and notes copyright © Sherrill Harbison, 1998
All rights reserved

LIBRARY OF CONGRESS CATALOGING-IN-PUBLICATION DATA
Undset, Sigrid, 1882-1949
   [Fortællingen om Viga-Ljot og Vigdis. English]
   Gunnar's daughter / Sigrid Undset ; translated by Arthur G. Chater ;
introduction and notes by Sherrill Harbison.
      p. cm.—(Penguin twentieth-century classics)
   ISBN 0 14 11.8020 X (pbk)
   1. Norway—History—1030–1397—Fiction   2 Iceland—History—To
1262—Fiction. 3 Middle Ages—History—Fiction. I. Chater,
Arthur G. II. Title. III. Series.
PT8950.U5F613   1998
839.8'2372—dc21   97-34337

Printed in the United States of America
Set in Bembo

Except in the United States of America, this book is sold subject to the condition
that it shall not, by way of trade or otherwise, be lent, resold, hired out, or otherwise
circulated without the publisher's prior consent in any form of binding or cover other
than that in which it is published and without a similar condition including
this condition being imposed on the subsequent purchaser

The scanning, uploading and distribution of this book via the Internet or via any
other means without the permission of the publisher is illegal and punishable by law.
Please purchase only authorized electronic editions, and do not participate in or encourage
electronic piracy of copyrighted materials Your support of the author's rights is appreciated.

CONTENTS

INTRODUCTION

Sigrid Undset's first historical novel, *Gunnar's Daughter* of 1909, is sometimes dismissed as a "saga pastiche," an apprentice work by a talented twenty-seven-year-old who would later ripen and produce her Nobel Prize–winning historical trilogy, *Kristin Lavransdatter*. Certainly in this early work Undset deliberately echoed both motifs and the spare prose and laconic tone of the thirteenth-century Icelandic sagas. But the novel is not an amateur exercise; it is simply different from its successors, and it is also different from anything else produced in its time. For unlike most of the Viking-inspired art of its period, *Gunnar's Daughter* is not a historical romance. It is a skillful conversation between two historical moments about questions as troublesome in Undset's own time—and in ours—as they were in the Saga Age: rape and revenge, civil and domestic violence, a troubled marriage, and children made victims of their parents' problems. Whether modern readers know Undset's saga models or not, they meet these themes in *Gunnar's Daughter* with a shock of recognition.

The novel, which was originally titled *Fortællingen om Viga-Ljot og Vigdis* (The Story of Viga-Ljot and Vigdis), is set in Norway and Iceland at the beginning of the eleventh century, the transition point between the Viking period and the Christian Middle Ages. Its narrative reads like a fairy tale repeatedly interrupted by reality. Vigdis Gunnarsdatter seems the classic princess, the beautiful, spoiled daughter of a wealthy and powerful father, when her suitor arrives from a distant land. But when the courtship begins, the fairy tale paradigm splits apart, and the book becomes a gripping psychological novel, a terse, swiftly moving tale of naive trust, betrayal, violation, and ven-

geance. Its extraordinary heroine is a woman toughened by
adversity and ennobled by courage, generosity, and clear judgment. After violence destroys her world and her prospects, Vigdis single-handedly rebuilds her life and restores her family's
honor, repeatedly defending her autonomy in a world governed
by men. But her most dangerous emotions are fanned by an
unremitting social code, and by acting in compliance with that
code she finally destroys her own happiness. *Gunnar's Daughter*
is a shocking story—not because the society it portrays is so
primitive, but because the issues and dilemmas it raises have
changed so little.

Sigrid Undset (1882–1949) was the third woman to be awarded
the Nobel Prize for Literature (1928). She was born in Ka-
lundborg, on the island of Sealand in Denmark, the first child
of Charlotte Gyth Undset, a Dane, and Ingvald Undset, a
young Norwegian archaeologist already prominent in his field.
The family moved permanently to Christiania (as Oslo was
called then) when Sigrid was two.

It was an auspicious time to grow up in the Norwegian
capital. At the conclusion of the Napoleonic wars in 1814 Denmark had been forced to give up its four-hundred-year rule of
Norway, which before being ceded to Sweden enjoyed a brief,
tantalizing taste of freedom. In the ensuing National Romantic
Movement (ca. 1844–72),[1] Norwegian historians, archaeolo-
gists, and artists sought to define a distinctive cultural identity
that would justify a return to full political independence.

History writing had not been an academic discipline very
long—only since the nineteenth-century democratic revolu-
tions throughout Europe had opened archives and documents
of state to public access for the first time. Most early histories
were designed to nourish increasingly strident nationalisms, and
Norway's were no exception. Artists and scholars, including the
folklorists Asbjørnson and Moe, the composer Grieg, the play-
wrights Ibsen and Bjørnson, and the painter J. C. Dahl, ex-

plored the Viking and medieval past in their work; many also fought to preserve native dialects and folklore, and to save the country's unique wooden stave churches from destruction.

Sigrid Undset's father had grown up in Trondheim, the seat of the medieval Norwegian kings, where Europe's northernmost Gothic cathedral was then undergoing restoration. Her grounding in the historical past began in her earliest years, when she learned to read Old Norse, visited archaeological sites, and learned from her father the rigorous, scientific approach to material that lent itself too easily to prettification and fantasy. She first recognized this scholarly ethic as an *aesthetic* during the summer she was ten years old, on a family visit to Trondheim. A family friend, noticing her boredom with her grandparents' library, handed her a copy of *Njals Saga*—the crown jewel of the thirteenth-century Icelandic sagas—with the comment "Let's see if you're grown up enough to get anything out of this."[2]

"After such an introduction obviously I couldn't give up on it," she recalled later, "even if reading the saga about Njal was quite a struggle at the beginning. But not for long." For days she lost track of everything else, rushing through breakfast to escape to the fields behind the house, where she stretched out in the sunshine to read. From time to time she had to push the book away and bury her face in the grass: "I could see it all so clearly that it hurt. Skarphedin, with his black eyes and pale face—beautiful eyes, but an ugly mouth—reckless, unpredictable"—she could not understand what was the matter with him. Whenever the others had achieved a reconciliation and everything seemed to be going well, Skarphedin, acting like a madman, came and destroyed it all.

The experience was like an earthquake, and the following winter she exhausted Petersen's translations of the sagas.[3] She was deeply affected by the individual portraits—Njal and Skarphedin in *Njals Saga*, Kjartan, Gudrun, and Bolli in *Laxdæla Saga*. These were psychological sketches and tales of personal tragedy, not mythic types; nor did the saga writers' sardonic humor, their cynicism about covetousness, vanity, and human aberration resemble folk legend.[4] This was history, surely, but history rendered with artistic vision.

The following year, when she was eleven, her father died after a long, debilitating illness. The family was left in considerable economic hardship, and throughout her adolescence Undset was depressed, lonely, and scornful of the world. At sixteen she quit school and went to work as a secretary for an engineering firm, where for the next decade she would support her mother and two younger sisters. That same year (1898) she answered an ad for a pen pal, and for the next six years a young Swedish woman named Dea Hedberg was the one confidante with whom Undset shared her sorrows, dreams, and her struggles as an aspiring writer.[5]

Undset knew very early that she wanted to write about the Middle Ages, but not in the romanticized manner of Walter Scott. She wanted to re-create what she had seen in the sagas, to write about human passions so *realistically*, she told Dea, that "everything that seems romantic from here—murder, violent episodes, etc., becomes ordinary—comes to life."[6] As a schoolchild she had seen one other model for what she was aiming at: the Bible stories, too, dealt with "real, living people—it was not disguised that although King David was a hero and a poet he was capable of mean actions, that the reckless Samson was considerably braver than he was wise, that the prophets could sulk and whine in their self-pity."[7]

To prepare for her task, Undset undertook a self-directed course of night (often all-night) study and writing after her full day at the office. She read widely in all periods of history and literature, both Norwegian and foreign, but especially from the Middle Ages. To her childhood legacy of Old Norse literature she now added *Minnesang*, legends and hagiography, theology and philosophy, epics and Continental romances.

In 1901 she reported a second earthquake: "I have discovered the book of my books and source of eternal life," she exclaimed to Dea. It was a collection of old Danish ballads, utterly different from any she knew. The Danish lords, far re-moved from the perfumed courtly world of the Continent, worked the plow themselves, and their deep love for home and their native soil struck her as instinctive and sensual, almost erotic. Thereafter she began to try, deliberately and painstak-ingly, to recapture their atmosphere in her own work.

Her first effort, begun in 1900 when she was eighteen, was a story set in Jutland in the fourteenth century, about a real historical character named Svend Trøst. Formal problems made the work grueling, as she felt the constant risk of attributing modern thoughts and feelings to characters from the year 1340. Months turned into years of labor, and she frequently vented her frustrations: "If you could see how I have worked on this, Dea! Only a few short chapters are the way I want them. This is the result of two years' trouble. And it's all madness, I can see it myself."[8]

Shortly afterward she set Svend Trøst aside to take up a different motif, set in the thirteenth century in the region of her birthplace in Denmark. This time, she told Dea, none of the characters would be based on historical people, "so that I will retain a free hand to let these folks do what comes to them naturally."[9] Still she had to struggle with historical accuracy, especially the language. To make it sound like everyday con-versation, but still have a tone of the past, she avoided any words not based on Old Danish. "But it's not easy, I can tell you—neither avoiding foreign words, nor getting the old words to fit smoothly, without affectation, pathos, or solem-nity."[10]

It was three more years before she had a satisfactory product, which she delivered to Gyldendal Publishing House in Copen-hagen in the summer of 1905.[11] There she received one of literature's most memorable rejections: "Don't try your hand at any more historical novels," advised editor Peter Nansen. "It's not your line. But you might, you know, try something modern. One can never tell!"[12] Undset took his advice as a challenge, and between 1907 and 1918 published eight volumes of fiction with contemporary settings. She put the medieval manuscript away, but did not forget it: twenty years later, reassured by the success of *Gunnar's Daughter* and *Kristin Lavransdatter*, she revised it as the story of Olav Audunsson, *The Master of Hestviken*. She had, in the interval, learned a good deal more about the Middle Ages, and also about her own time.

Just a few months after her rejection at Gyldendal in 1905, a major historical event stirred her country's national pride: Sweden peacefully relinquished its hold on Norway, granting the country full independence for the first time since the fourteenth century. In some circles, nationalist feeling became not less but more intense after sovereignty was achieved, fanning romantic enthusiasm for the heroic age of the Vikings. By now, though, interest in the Nordic past was part of a larger European curiosity about primitivism of many kinds.

Perhaps the simplest way to describe the general crisis in European intellectual life at the time Undset began her literary career is with the term "evolutionary panic"—which was as much a fear about the future of the human race as uneasiness about its past. If entire species had died out over time, how could human survival—human progress—be guaranteed? From now on, some reasoned, evolution ought not to be left to chance; careful breeding could give humanity more control over the direction of the species in the future. In that interest scientists puzzled over tribal behavior on distant continents, and measured skulls, recorded dreams, and dissected bodies close to home. Philosophers rushed to reinterpret the history of ancient civilizations, looking both for signs of hereditary vigor and for decadence and decay, wondering which trends to encourage in their own time, and which to fear.[13]

At the turn of the century a widespread decline in the European birthrate—Norway included—alarmed many. Could this be a sign of the end of civilization? To those who deplored the ennui and "effeteness" of Decadence, the energy and enterprise of the rugged pagan past seemed attractive, the Viking achievement evidence of the "true greatness" of the Nordic race. The same theme had already been explored by the composer Richard Wagner, whose massive musical reinterpretations of Nordic myths had an immense cult following.

A key concept of the post-Darwin era was positivism, the idea that the world could be improved through science. And to men bent on scientifically controlling the future of the race, growing female autonomy—particularly the "New Woman" who chose a career over marriage—seemed threatening. Artists of the period reflected this widespread *fin de siècle* misogyny both in sentimental paeans to female innocence and motherhood, and in images of malevolent viragos and seductresses (Salome was particularly popular), whose "unnatural" traits threatened to contaminate the gene pool.

Like some others of her generation, Sigrid Undset found much of this distasteful and alarming. The notion that women were merely breeders of the super-race, with no erotic appetites or intellectual interests of their own, seemed to revert to the pagan Saga Age, when marriages were arranged by men in the interest of controlling kinship relations. As for the perceived "threat" of female independence, she well knew that all women were not cut out to be mothers, and believed that, for children's sake, they should have opportunities better suited to their temperaments. She also knew from personal experience that not all women in the workplace were there voluntarily. Industrialism and poverty forced many women into situations where their labor—and their innocence—were exploited in hostile and unsafe environments. She had already made the dislocation of such young women, whose loneliness made them easy prey for sexual predators, the theme of some of her modern stories.[14]

Most dangerous of all, however, was the nationalist tendency toward isolationist race mythology. It was crucially important, Undset believed, to understand the country's history in the larger European context. A glorified image of the Vikings obscured the fact that they had not been peaceful, diplomatic cultural ambassadors but brutal marauders, raiding, destroying, killing, and abducting innocent people.

Increasingly, Undset felt she recognized in her own day the same dilemma that faced Icelandic society in the Saga Age, only in reverse. She was concerned to see growing admiration for brute force give rise to mystical cults worshiping instinct, vitality, youth, and "life force," which showed striking parallels to the Viking ethic of the right of the stronger. In the Middle Ages the pagan code of vigilante justice, which rested on superior strength, had eventually been eclipsed by a philosophy that acknowledged the value and dignity of every individual, whether weak or strong. Now, it appeared, the world was returning to heathen times, with virulent forms of narcissism, chauvinism, and positivist arrogance eclipsing the teachings of compassion, mercy, and protection of the weak. As if to confirm her fears, in 1907 her compatriot and fellow novelist Knut Hamsun—who would also win the Nobel Prize—publicly advocated neglect of the elderly as state policy. Because old people were unproductive and dwelt in the past, he claimed, public resources should instead be channeled toward vigorous, forward-looking youth.

Gunnar's Daughter, published two years after Hamsun's incendiary speech, was not only the first proof of Undset's long years of apprenticeship in writing historical fiction. It was also her first artistic statement about the disturbing link she saw between ancient and modern paganisms. A few years later she would begin to battle Hamsun's views—views that led him eventually to the Nazi party—more publicly and directly.[15]

Late in 1909 Sigrid Undset wrote to Dea Hedberg, "My new book is another success; it seems like the biggest." *Gunnar's Daughter* aroused great curiosity about its twenty-seven-year-old author, and in her first published interview the following spring, Undset was asked why a modern young woman from

Christiania would choose to write about such barbarism, and to do so in the archaic style of the Saga Age. It was a period she felt sure she understood, she replied, because there, society's structures were so simple that what was "pure and unmediated in human nature"—the strong, unruly passions such as desire, jealousy, pride, compassion, greed—lay fully exposed. And the archaic style was not just a veneer over dead ideas, but a concise artistic form used to reflect thoughts and feelings common to people of all ages. Of course, she warned, no one should literally attempt to write sagas today. But if one "peels off" the intellectual framework of the modern era, she explained,

> one steps straight into the Middle Ages, and can see life from its point of view. It comes together with one's own. And if one tries to report exactly what one has seen, the forms will be related involuntarily. And one writes as a contemporary. One can, of course, only write novels about one's contemporary time.[16]

This comment—judiciously silent about the five years she had worked to make old and new forms *appear* to be "related involuntarily"—was only partly disingenuous. Of course she was writing, and understood she was writing, about her own century. But she also had felt at home in the Middle Ages since childhood, and did feel that she wrote from its point of view. "I think . . . that the reason why I understand our own time so well," she wrote to a friend in 1919, "is because ever since I was a child I have had some kind of living memories from an earlier age to compare with it."[17] It is her conviction of this—and her compelling distillation of the saga writers' style—that draws readers with her into that earlier age.

What was this age in which Undset felt so much at home?
It was a period of about five hundred years, beginning in 874, when a group of restless, disaffected Norwegian families

began leaving home to settle on Iceland, and lasting until the fourteenth century, when their descendants brought their historical chronicle up to date. Although the Icelanders' achievements and exploits were remarkable from the start—they established a republican form of government, an anomaly in the Middle Ages, and their superior seamanship led them to explore North America before the first millennium—no one wrote about them at all during their first century, because Old Norse culture was nonliterate. Norsemen used an ancient runic alphabet for short inscriptions or magical incantations (like those scratched on the handle of Vigdis Gunnarsdatter's "priestess's knife" in Undset's novel). But the elaborate historical, legal, mythic, and artistic traditions were all memorized and transmitted orally. It was this preliterate period, known as the Saga Age, that most captured the imagination of thirteenth- and nineteenth-century historians alike.

What we know about Scandinavia at that time comes from two kinds of sources: archaeology, art, runic inscriptions, and contemporary accounts written by foreign visitors; and later native literary sources, including myth, poetry, laws, and the sagas, all derived from oral tradition, but none recorded until after Christianity had provided the tool of literacy and otherwise left its imprint on the culture. Of these sources, the sagas (saga, or "that which is said," refers to any prose narrative) are the fullest and richest in detail, but because most were written centuries after the events they describe, their accuracy must be weighed carefully.

Two features of Old Norse culture distinguished it from the rest of medieval Europe: its legal system, which endorsed ritualized blood feud, and the role and status of Norse women, who struck foreign visitors as startlingly autonomous and powerful. The role of women was related to the vengeance code in ways that were obscure to outsiders, and during the period in which the North was Christianized, both features underwent very gradual, but very fundamental, change.

The disgruntled chieftains who set out for Iceland in the

ninth century disliked the increasing centralization of power in Norway, which was moving for the first time toward monarchy. In their new home they exercised their authority as they had before, in local assemblies *(things),* which served legal, business, and social functions. In 930 the Icelanders organized as a commonwealth, and citizens met annually at an *Althing.*

As an independent republic with no executive authority, Icelandic society was unusually preoccupied with the task of maintaining law and order. A chief purpose of the gatherings at the *thing* was to provide peer mediation for civic and criminal complaints, either by agreeing on a suitable fine *(weregild)* or by banishing (outlawing) the offenders. Because personal reputation or honor was the basis of influence and power, defamation of character—any accusation of weakness or error—could prove the most serious kind of offense. As it could be considered shameful to accept blood money for one's kin, settlements by *weregild* did not always end a dispute, and if no peaceful agreement could be reached by mediation, blood vengeance was the recognized recourse. (Examples of all these kinds of dilemmas arise in *Gunnar's Daughter*).

The right of revenge usually fell to the victim's male kin. Should a woman feel her family's honor imperfectly redeemed, she could goad or incite the men to further action. If she were the sole heir to a dishonor, however, the avenging deed could itself devolve on her.[18] This sacred duty of revenge meant that "masculine" virtues—willpower, courage, and physical strength—were awarded the highest value in both men *and* women. To develop these qualities youths were trained in determination, bravery, skill with weapons, and stoic patience and self-control. Patience and self-control were imperative because blood vengeance was a moral responsibility, not simply an indulgence of ill feeling—immediate retaliation motivated by rage was considered cowardly and dishonorable. Vengeance had to be exacted with care, preferably in a memorable and dramatic manner that would be told to future generations. Since family honor was more important than individual life, the brave could welcome death in the assurance that their kin would honor them with a "good revenge."

Such imperatives left their mark on the character of the entire population, and it was this apparent imperviousness to sentiment that most consistently impressed foreign observers. Their reports of assertive Nordic women were also, of course, colored by their own cultural norms and political objectives. Eighth- and ninth-century visitors from Moorish Spain and the Middle East—accustomed to the veil and the harem—were astonished by the sight of tall, blond, bare-limbed women in free movement. They were impressed that Viking noblewomen could be military leaders, that ordinary women could command great wealth, had the right to divorce, and could, as one observer reported, cast unwanted infants into the sea.[19]

Norse women did have some rights not available to women in the southern countries. The society provided for bilateral descent and inheritance (though males got the larger portion).[20] A wife could divorce her husband for failure to provide economic support, for attempting to confiscate her property, and for physical abuse, homosexuality, or incest.[21] When a marriage was dissolved, women took their property with them, which gave them important leverage in marital disputes.

But the picture was not all rosy. Women in Old Norse society had no say in their marriages, which were considered a commercial and political contract between male parties; they were valued chiefly as bearers of children who would extend the family's sphere of influence. Men were permitted concubines, which made sexual jealousy and rivalry between offspring potentially constant features of domestic life. And although physical hardiness was necessary in the rigorous Scandinavian climate, women were trained in "manly" stoicism because the murder of loved ones was something to be expected, part of the justice system, and because they might themselves inherit the dangerous obligation of revenge.

The haunting image of women casting infants into the sea (also mentioned in *Gunnar's Daughter*) neglects to tell that in this society men, not women, had the right to decide whether a newborn should be raised or disposed of. The decision, which fell to the father or the woman's male relatives, was based on a range of factors, including legitimacy, questionable paternity, the family's ability to provide, superstitions connected with conception or delivery, and the infant's appearance, frailty, deformity—or sex. As in all bellicose cultures, male infants were valued more highly than females, and the startlingly low ratio of adult females to males in grave finds from the pre-Christian period strongly supports the likelihood of preferential female infanticide throughout Scandinavia.[22]

Christian missionaries too described Norse women according to their own values and objectives, which were more self-interested than those of Arab merchants. As clerics bent on replacing pagan laws with ecclesiastical authority, they discouraged power competitions among rival families and promoted the strange new ideal of chivalry, where a man's noble status was no longer measured by his cunning and physical prowess, but by his defense of the weak and respect for female chastity. In his Latin history of Denmark, *Gesta Danorum* (ca. 1200), the cleric Saxo Grammaticus wrote disapprovingly of "maiden warriors" of pagan times, who were "forgetful of their true selves" and "put toughness before allure." "Loathing a dainty style of living," he scolded, "they would harden body and mind with toil and endurance," courting military celebrity "so earnestly that you would have guessed they had unsexed themselves." Forgetting what he called their "true selves," they "put toughness before allure, aimed at conflicts rather than kisses, . . . fitted to weapons hands that should have been weaving, desired not the couch but the kill."[23]

Saxo's hostility to women who seemed indifferent to male protection reflects his ignorance of their living conditions, as well as the clerical misogyny that undermined much of Gospel teaching about equality of the sexes; it also bears a striking resemblance to cultural images of aggressive women in Undset's own generation. Since Saxo was writing two centuries after the introduction of Christianity, he drew his "maiden warrior" images not from personal observation but from old literary sources, chiefly heroic poetry. Two legends, both preserved in the Poetic Edda (1270), suggest prototypes for his rendering of Old Norse femininity. In the *Lay of Atli*, Atli (the Hun Attila) kills his wife Gudrun's brothers in a dispute. In return, she not only kills her husband, but first kills their two sons and feeds him their hearts. The second example is the "Helgi Poems," which tell of the hero Helgi's love for the Valkyrie Sigrun. Helgi kills the rival king to whom Sigrun's father had betrothed her, together with her father and brother. Another brother carries out vengeance against Helgi, and in the last poem, the grieving Sigrun spends a last night with Helgi's ghost in his burial mound.

Both stories illustrate the classic dilemma of women in the heroic age, torn between obligations to their lovers and their families of origin.[24] The first poem, which comes from an older source than the second, makes clear Gudrun's distress at what she has done (she tries to drown herself), but the grisly deed is understood as a terrible but necessary result of the crimes committed against her kin. Sigrun's dilemma is much like Gudrun's, but she transfers her loyalty from her father to her lover. This reflects a changed sensibility, an interest in female dilemmas and emotions not part of the earlier culture, and the difference of emphasis reflects the same changing value system we see beginning to form in *Gunnar's Daughter*.

The long, slow process of change was inaugurated by Norway's first Christian king, Olav Trygvesson, who plays a small but critical role in *Gunnar's Daughter*. The colorful Olav was a magnetic leader who had been baptized on one of his viking adventures in Britain, and during the five years of his reign (995–1000) he made it his mission to Christianize his homeland. In doing so he used familiar slash-and-burn methods—as Undset once put it, he received Christianity "in the same way that a Viking entered the service of a more powerful king, and his object was to lay Norway as booty at the feet of Christ."[25]

(In *Gunnar's Daughter*, Vigdis echoes this pagan attitude toward might and power, remarking that it was a "strange religion" whose God allowed himself to be slain by his enemies.)

By far the greatest change effected by the conversion of the North was the introduction of written script to the culture. Clergy arrived to establish monasteries and Latin schools, and brought with them secular literature from the Continent as well as sacred texts. Native-born clerics soon adapted written script to the Norse language, and began writing out the lives of Christian saints, followed by their own laws and histories. Thus was oral tradition filtered through the double prisms of the new faith and Latin literary forms.

Among the most difficult cultural adjustments brought by the church were those affecting marriage and women's rights. The Christian marriage, modeled on Christ's mystical marriage with the church, was regarded not as contract but as a sacrament, and a woman's consent was required for it to be valid. Consent protected women (in theory at least) from unwanted unions; it also gave them recourse to legal support from the bishop or the crown. The church also provided them an alternative: women who chose to go to a convent could not be forced into any marriage. Most radical, perhaps, was the Christian expectation of lifelong monogamy and fidelity from both marriage partners, outlawing the sexual double standard. This last, Undset once observed, was so novel a requirement and so fundamentally opposed to the customs of the time that Saint Olav himself did not abide by it.[26] But throughout the Northern world the regulations worked gradually in the interest of more affective marriages, laying the groundwork for the medieval cult of romantic love, which was immensely popular with women.[27]

After conversion, commerce and cultural exchange with the Continent gradually replaced Viking piracy, and study in Europe and travel to the Holy Land became fashionable. In Iceland in the thirteenth century, however, feuds between rival factions again terrorized the populace. After an appeal for help, the country was annexed by the Norwegian crown in 1262, and blood feuds were outlawed under Norwegian law. In 1303 all special privileges of the republic were revoked, and the island was reduced to a dependency.

It was during these turbulent and heartbreaking years that the bulk of Iceland's literary tradition was committed to writing in the sagas, and most of what we know about Norwegian and Icelandic history up to that time is due to this remarkable literary flowering. The saga writers—most of whom are anonymous—had complex concerns. As Icelanders, they were inspired by their own heritage and sympathetic to its continued importance to their families and neighbors. Insofar as they were Christian clerics, they wanted to reflect the teachings of their faith. And because they were members of a proud nation threatened with extinction, their desire to celebrate what was peculiar to their tradition was intensified. All of these interests are represented—some anachronistically—in the sagas about the past.

The thirteenth century may be designated the classic age of the sagas. Snorri Sturlason's *Heimskringla*, or *History of the Kings of Norway* (1230), belongs to the group of "kings' sagas," the only ones including known authors, which are the basis of the Norwegian historical tradition. Snorri's tale begins as far back as the reign of the semilegendary Ynglings and extends to 1177, with the bulk of it devoted to biographies of the two great Olavs, King Olav Trygvesson and the younger King Olav Haraldsson (the Saint).

The so-called family sagas, of which there are about thirty, are the pride of Icelandic literature. They are chiefly an account of Iceland's settlement and the gradual growth of the new community, focusing on genealogy, tales of remarkable deeds, bitter feuds between rival chieftains, and portraits of memorable persons. Because their historical accounts—culled from both oral tradition and living memory—are interlaced with elements of myth and apocryphal embellishment, both the kings' sagas and family sagas are best classified as historical fiction. A third group is the "fiction sagas," or, as the Icelanders called them, the "lying sagas," which were understood to be pure entertainment, not history. Included in this group are the so-called knights' sagas, which corresponded to the increasingly popular imported chivalric romances.

By common consensus, what is most plainly revealed in all the sagas is the blending of indigenous Norse culture with imported European thinking. This blend is very clear in the two most important models for *Gunnar's Daughter*, *Njals Saga* and the *Laxdæla Saga*, from which Undset borrowed specific motifs, language, and tone. *Njals Saga*, written about three hundred years after Iceland's conversion, is the story of the pagan lawsayer Njal, who oversees the country's transition from pagan to Christian law in the year 1000. Throughout the tale the author demonstrates his admiration for both the pagan virtues of honor, fortitude, and physical prowess, and the Christian emphasis on goodwill, humility, and conciliation. When Flosi and his henchmen surround and set fire to Njal's homestead, for example, they temper the deed with a Christian gesture and offer those inside a free exit. Njal elects to remain, however, and die a noble death, explaining that he is too old to continue the cycle of vengeance, but he cannot "live in shame."[28] His wife and grandson choose to die with him. Njal's heroism thus becomes Christian martyrdom, and Christian justice prevails at the end, when Flosi goes on a pilgrimage to Rome, receives absolution from the pope, and returns home to be reconciled to his enemies.

The *Laxdæla Saga* (ca. 1270) provides a transition between the family and "lying" sagas by reflecting another change of sensibility introduced by Christianity—an appeal to the interests and psychology of women. The *Laxdæla* is the only saga to have a woman as its main character. It also has the broadest range of female personalities, including a pioneer settler and matriarch of a dynasty, a slave who is really a princess, a woman who "wears breeches" and takes vengeance with the sword, another who forces her deserting husband to take responsibility for his child. Gudrun Osvifsdottir, the memorable heroine, is a beauty who marries four times but loves only once. In jealousy she exacts a cruel revenge on the man she loves, and breaks her own heart in the process. She ends her life as the first anchoress in Iceland.

Although it belongs to the group of family sagas, the *Laxdæla* was clearly influenced by the Continental romances, the first of which (Thomas's *Tristan*) was translated to Old Norse in 1226. The foreign genre presented an entirely new concept of the hero: he was not just valiant and strong, but a sensitive soul who wept and sighed, and his purpose was not the defense of his kin but the quest of a bride. Woman was no longer merely a property asset; she was the object of desire, and for Norsemen, proving one's manhood by winning a woman's favor required new, highly unfamiliar strategies.[29]

The paradigm of the bridal-quest romances, of which *Tristan* is the archetype, is still familiar today in fairy tales: a youth decides to woo a maiden, and makes an expedition to win her favor. He encounters multiple obstacles, but finally overcomes all and wins his bride. As already noted, *Gunnar's Daughter* follows the familiar chivalric model—at first. But then the story spins out of control, and at critical moments both Ljot and Vigdis resort to the violence of the old vengeance code. While revenge is cathartic, it also destroys love, hope, and romance.

The theme of most of the sagas, Undset later wrote, was the conflict "between a man's propriety and his convictions, between his conscience and the ethical demands of his society." "Now one might well think," she continued,

> that in these tightly organized blood relationships, where it was the duty of the richest and strongest to protect the family members who were less fortunate, where the old and the orphaned were guaranteed help in the family, and where glory or praise connected with one cast its reflection over the whole group—

that all this would give the single individual a feeling of security, and increase his joy in life. But such is not the case in the sagas. There we see, almost without exception, that this mutual dependence made men and women feel trapped, that through it they were forced into unlucky or tragic or ridiculous situations. . . . These obligations could compel an honorable man to do many things that he himself knew were wrong—that went against his new Christian conscience. . . . It is such conflicts that the saga writers read out of the tales from older days.[30]

In pagan times, in other words, social rules and expectations—though harsh—were clear and without personal conflict. It was the clash of cultural values—the radically *reversed* concepts of honor and virtue introduced by Christianity—that created so much strain and confusion in the old culture. But whereas the thirteenth-century saga writers had wanted to show their pagan ancestors *positively,* and thus injected modern Christian ethics into their accounts of blood feuds, Undset wanted to show the pagan period *negatively,* because she feared the revival of sanctified violence in her own time. This is one reason the church plays little evident role in the tempering of Viga-Ljot. He first sees his many misfortunes as being linked not to his own bad behavior, but to Vigdis's curse. When he finally does accept his own responsibility, he becomes more humane and faithful to those entrusted to his care. Although his baptism had been more a matter of courtesy than conviction, he observes the new laws against adultery and child exposure, and his sacrifice for his son's sake—and to stop the cycle of violence—is more like Njal's Christian martyrdom in the saga than like Gunnar's pagan pride earlier in Undset's novel.

Vigdis too feels the conflict of values, and like many of the moral conflicts reported in the sagas, hers suggest Christian influence anachronistically. One is the conflict between her own attraction to Ljot and her need to defend her family's honor, which Ljot has compromised. This suggestion of romantic love between Ljot and Vigdis—like that of Gudrun for Kjartan in the *Laxdæla Saga*—reflects attitudes toward marriage and love that entered Norse culture only with the Continental romances, two centuries after Vigdis's story takes place. More true to her own era, Vigdis elects to meet her bloody obligation, making it clear that the new religion has made even less impression on her than it had on Ljot. Only King Olav's respect for her rights and dignity had ever caused her to think well of Christianity, and as the narrative relates, "she was not very zealous in the faith, for she had much to see to on her estate." It is largely this lack of impression that leaves an impression on the reader.

In her deep probing of Vigdis's second, even more serious conflict, however, Undset breaks with saga tradition. This is the conflict between Vigdis's love for her son and her consuming personal rage, which, after all her years of waiting and plotting the mandated "perfect" revenge, still takes over her reason. Undset's extraordinary portrayal in this early novel (1909!) of the fear, self-loathing, suicidal depression, loss of trust, and blinding fury that permanently change the lives of rape victims has no literary equal until late in the twentieth century. In writing about this subject, and doing so in almost clinical detail, Undset was remarkably ahead of her time.

Reading *Gunnar's Daughter* today is an experience comprising at least five literary/historical layers. Our understanding of the tenth-century pagan Norse world comes chiefly through histories written by thirteenth-century Icelanders, using their own language modified by Latin literary forms, in narratives that convey both admiration for their pagan ancestors and affirmations of their own medieval Christian values. At the turn of the twentieth century, Undset echoed the saga writers' mood, filtered now through modern Dano-Norwegian[31] and her concerns about the violence and racial arrogance of her own era. The novel was translated into English in 1936, while—confirming Undset's fears—fascist troops gathered in Europe and Hitler prepared his blueprint for the master race. English archaisms were now stirred into the already studied linguistic mix of Old Norse, Latin, medieval Icelandic, and modern Norwegian.

Today, more than sixty years later, readers bring to the novel knowledge of violence on a scale unimaginable in 1909 or 1936, including the Holocaust and the threat of nuclear annihilation. They also bring social views considerably affected by feminist and multicultural perspectives. Why, then, does the violence in *Gunnar's Daughter* still have such power to shock? What can we learn from it about the past? About ourselves?

We can learn a good deal about the Saga Age from the novel, because although modern research has added depth and detail to our picture of the Old Norse world, Undset's scholarship remains fundamentally sound. We can also get a taste of the sagas' pungent style through her later echo of it. Her syntax is marked by its Icelandic models in matters of verb and subject arrangement, adjectival description, and the predominate use of coordinating clauses. She also adopts the sagas' vivid realism; their cynical, ironic tone, conveyed largely through understatement; their sharp characterizations, effected chiefly through dialogue; and their wealth of detail about everyday life, including portraits of children unique in medieval literature—indeed without parallel until the nineteenth century.

Gunnar's Daughter also borrows thematic details—too many to mention—from the sagas. Elements of Ljot's physical appearance and impulsive character are drawn from Skarphedin in *Njals Saga*; the horse fight and the burning of the aged Gunnar and his consort come from the same source. Vigdis's lifelong obsession with Ljot's treachery and her final confession to her son have parallels in the story of Gudrun Osvifsdottir in the *Laxdæla Saga*.[32] The easy, informal relation between King Olav Trygvesson and his subjects is prefigured in the *Laxdæla*, as are the hauntings by the ghosts of Ljot's children, Leikny's attraction to a nunnery, the saga-within-the-saga of Vigdis's foster mother, Æsa, and the important gift of a red embroidered cloak.

The sagas were not Undset's only source, however. She was well aware that, like the Vikings, the Old Testament kings raided and destroyed to prove their strength and prowess; there is also an important echo of the death of Saul in this story. From medieval legends and hagiography she borrowed symbolic motifs—saints Agatha and Margaret, for example, mentioned only in passing, were both third-century virgin martyrs who lost their lives defending their chastity.

The novel also borrows elements from folk ballads, the Nordic variant of chivalric poetry. Ljot's undying fidelity to the memory of his first love is a chivalric ethic that would not have been understood by the pagan culture. At least twenty Scandinavian ballads tell (though certainly not in Undset's manner) about the rape or attempted rape of a maiden,[33] a theme that has no parallel in the sagas. Some of the ballads' rhythmic vigor is incorporated in Undset's short, trenchant sentences.[34]

What speaks most eloquently in Undset's own twentieth-century voice, however, is the novel's focus on sexual violence. Vigdis's most profound injury is not the loss of Gunnar; indeed, his death in defense of family honor was itself honorable, and to be expected. It is rather her loss of innocence and trust in the man she wanted to love, and her subjection, as the weaker of two parties, to physical force. This is the first sign of the novel's modernity, since innocence and trust—though expected of young women in Undset's day—could hardly have lasted past childhood in a blood-feud society. In this regard, Vigdis's feelings are very unheroic, less like ancient shame than a very modern, very personal feminist fury.

The plot of her vendetta also suggests modern anxiety. The Salome motif in this novel reflects not just its biblical source, but its wide popularity with Undset's contemporaries. In the hands of male artists—Flaubert, Wilde, Beardsley, Richard Strauss—the theme conveyed the intense misogyny of the pe-

riod, but in the hands of a female artist—one exemplifying the economically independent New Woman whom many men found so alarming—it represents quite different feelings.[35]

The subject of this novel, like that of all Undset's historical fiction, is the effect of human passions on social order, the point at which intimate relations and social justice intersect. To obtain information about these things she consulted laws, legends, and religious writings of the past. The very debates recorded there—about criminal behavior, the position of women, marriage customs, infanticide, medical practices, social taboos, and the role of religion in everyday life—were the most vexing ones in the transition between the pagan and Christian cultures, which is why laws and legends were written about them in the first place.

We face the same dilemma today, of course. At the end of the second millennium—which many philosophers already describe as the post-Christian era—the issues that provoke the most ·vehement debates include civil and domestic violence, divorce and alternative family arrangements, illegitimacy, child custody, abortion, euthanasia, and the relation between church and state—the same issues the Icelanders struggled with a millennium ago. In our time as in theirs, shifts in these customs threaten long-held religious values, and so meet with great resistance. Undset understood how long it took for such fundamental changes to be absorbed; three centuries after Vigdis takes revenge on Ljot, the life of Olav Audunsson, her *Master of Hestviken*, comes undone over the same issue.

It is, finally, her focus on such intractable moral questions that makes Undset's medieval novels, despite their historical settings, seem so eerily modern—that and her unflinching honesty in probing the motives, delusions, and determinations of what she called the "human heart." For while she conveys enormous sympathy for Vigdis as a victim of violence, Undset refuses to sentimentalize her—or any of her characters. She understands that being badly used does not make one a saint, but only a badly used person bearing permanent scars and deep resentments. Without social structures to provide justice, reconciliation is impossible, and unreconciled pain and anger can lead victims to victimize others. This psychological acuity, combined with Undset's historical astuteness and a felicitous style, helps modern readers share her illusion of being "contemporary" with characters living a thousand years in the past.

Sherrill Harbison
Amherst, Massachusetts
September 1997

NOTES TO INTRODUCTION

1. These dates coincide with the reigns of Swedish kings Oscar I and Karl XV. The movement officially ended with the so-called Modern Breakthrough, a movement for realism and social relevance in Scandinavian literature inaugurated by the Danish critic Georg Brandes in 1871.

2. Sigrid Undset, "En bok som blev et vendepunkt i mitt liv" (A Book That Was a Turning Point in My Life), in *Artikler og essays om litteratur*, ed. Jan Fr. Daniloff (Oslo: H. Aschehoug, 1986), p. 300 (hereafter cited as "Vendepunkt").

3. Borghild Krane, *Sigrid Undset, liv og meninger* (Oslo: Gyldendal, 1970), p. 33.

4. Sigrid Undset, "Vendepunkt," p. 302.

5. Most of Undset's letters to Dea were preserved and published as *Kjære Dea*, foreword by Christianne Undset Svarstad (Oslo: J. W. Cappelen, 1979).

6. Sigrid Undset, *Kjære Dea*, p. 82.

7. Sigrid Undset, in "Omkring Abrahams offer" (On the Sacrifice of Abraham). Liv Bliksrud, ed., *Kritikk og tro. Tekster av Sigrid Undset* (Oslo: St. Olav Forlag, 1982), p. 98.

8. Sigrid Undset, *Kjære Dea*, p. 67.

9. Ibid., p. 85.

10. Ibid., p. 91.

11. The hegemony of Danish publishers in Norway was a long time breaking, and in 1905 Gyldendal was perhaps the most prestigious Danish company (the Norwegian affiliate, Gyldendal Norsk, did not break away from Co-

penhagen until 1925). When Undset did make her
publishing breakthrough, it was with Gyldendal's Norwegian rival, H. Aschehoug & Co.

12. A. H. Winsnes, *Sigrid Undset: A Study in Christian Realism*,
trans. P. G. Foote (London: Sheed & Ward, 1953), p. 34.

13. For an account of the development of these ideas see
George Stocking, *Victorian Anthropology* (New York: Macmillan, 1987).

14. Both the title story and "En fremmed" (A Stranger) from
Undset's untranslated 1908 collection *Den lykkelige alder*
(The Happy Age) treat this theme. It would reappear in
Jenny (1911, translated 1921), which scandalized the Nor-
wegian reading public.

15. Knut Hamsun (1859–1952), who won the Nobel Prize
in 1920, was Sigrid Undset's senior by a generation. His
notorious speech "Ærer de unge" (Honor the Young)
was delivered to the University Student Union in Christiania on April 27, 1907, and first published in the journal
Politiken in January 1912. Undset responded directly to it
in a 1914 address to the Student Union of the Trondheim
Technical College. In "Det fjerde bud" (The Fourth
Commandment) she discussed the value of experience
and old-age wisdom. The speech was included in her
1919 collection of essays titled *Et kvinnesynspunkt* (A
Woman's Point of View) (Oslo: H. Aschehoug, 1982).

16. Interview in *Urd*, 1910, cited in Borghild Krane, *Sigrid
Undset, liv og meninger*, p. 33.

17. Letter to Nini Roll Anker, cited by A. H. Winsnes, *Sigrid
Undset*, p. 2.

18. Carol Clover, "Maiden Warriors and Other Sons," *Journal of English and Germanic Philology*, vol. 85, no. 1
(January 1986).

19. These were the reactions of the southern visitors Al-
Ghazal, a ninth-century Andalusian poet and philosopher;
Ibrahim b. Ya'qub al-Turtushi, a tenth-century merchant
from Muslim Spain; and Ibn Fadlan, a diplomat from

Baghdad, also in the tenth century. See Judith Jesch, *Women in the Viking Age* (Woodbridge, England: Boydell Press, 1991).

20. Birgit and Peter Sawyer, *Medieval Scandinavia: From Conversion to Reformation, circa 800–1500* (Minneapolis: University of Minnesota Press, 1993).

21. Jenny Jochens, *Women in Old Norse Society* (Ithaca and London: Cornell University Press, 1995), pp. 55–57.

22. See Carol Clover, "The Politics of Scarcity: Notes on the Sex Ratio in Early Scandinavia," in *New Readings on Women in Old English Literature*, ed. Helen Damico and Alexandra Hennessey Olsen (Bloomington: Indiana University Press, 1990); also Birgit and Peter Sawyer, *Medieval Scandinavia*.

23. Judith Jesch, *Women in the Viking Age*, p. 176.

24. Judith Jesch analyzes the two poems in *Women in the Viking Age*, pp. 142–47 and 169–73.

25. Sigrid Undset, *Saga of Saints*, trans. E. C. Ramsden (New York: Longmans, Green, 1934), p. 56.

26. Ibid., p. 111.

27. Judith Jesch points out that the demanding physical and psychic regimen required by Old Norse society hints at the enormous cost of constant vigilance to social stability and domestic life, suggesting one probable reason that Norse women converted to Christianity earlier, in greater numbers, and with greater enthusiasm than men (*Women in the Viking Age*, pp. 197–200). See also Birgit and Peter Sawyer, *Medieval Scandinavia*, pp. 197–99.

28. Compare *Njals Saga*, Chapter 129.

29. For a history of this type in saga literature see Marianne Kalinke, *Bridal-Quest Romance in Medieval Iceland* (Ithaca: Cornell University Press, 1990).

30. Sigrid Undset, "Vendepunkt," pp. 305–6.

31. When Norway was separated from Denmark in 1814, it had been part of the kingdom of Denmark-Norway for more than four hundred years. Though the majority of

the rural population spoke dialects derived from Old
Norse, Norway did not have its own national language;
the official written language was Danish. Furthermore,
there were no Norwegian universities until 1811, so Danish influence on Norwegian pronunciation and usage was
perpetuated by both the educated and ruling classes. During the National Romantic Movement the self-taught
peasant schoolteacher Ivar Aasen launched a major effort
to institutionalize a "purified" Norwegian language, derived from folk dialects and free of Danish influence. The
folk language (first called *landsmål,* or "country speech,"
and in 1929 renamed *Nynorsk,* or "new Norwegian") was
officially given equal recognition in 1885, and it won
some important literary converts, including Arne Garborg
and Olav Duun. The so-called language wars, debates
about which language should predominate, were bitter for
a good many years, but Dano-Norwegian retained its
hold, partly because of its use by the influential play-
wrights Ibsen and Bjørnson. Undset, who was proud
of her own Danish heritage, also stayed with Dano-
Norwegian.

Today both languages are still official and are required
subjects in school, but since 1942 the influence of *Nynorsk*
as a competing language has declined, while its influence
on developing modern Norwegian has grown. See Einar
Haugen, *The Scandinavian Languages: An Introduction to
Their History* (London: Faber and Faber, 1976).

32. Compare Gudrun to her son Bolli: "I was worst to the
    one I loved most." *Laxdœla Saga,* translation and intro-
    duction by Magnus Magnusson and Hermann Pålsson
    (Baltimore: Penguin, 1969), p. 238.

33. Most of these ballads are Danish, a few Norwegian. See
    the descriptive catalogue published by the Institute for
    Comparative Research in Human Cultures, Oslo, *The
    Types of the Scandinavian Medieval Ballad* (Oslo/Bergen/
    Tromsø: Universitetsforlaget, 1978), pp. 121–27.

34. For a discussion of Undset's adaptation of medieval usage see Einar Haugen, *Norwegian Word Studies*, vol. 1: *On the Vocabularies of Sigrid Undset and Ivar Aasen* (Madison: University of Wisconsin Press, 1942).

35. Compare the 1900 tapestry by the Norwegian designer Frida Hansen, a large work titled *The Dance of Salome*, which depicts Salome and Herodias flanked by female attendants; it includes no male figures at all. See *Lost Paradise: Symbolist Europe*, exhibition catalogue (Montreal: Montreal Museum of Fine Arts, 1995), p. 396.

SUGGESTIONS FOR FURTHER READING

Many of Undset's early works remain untranslated, and most of the literature about her is in Norwegian. This list is designed around four themes: Undset's own writing about the Middle Ages; critical studies of her historical fiction bearing relevance to *Gunnar's Daughter*; the late Viking period in which the novel is set, with special attention to women's history; and the literary-cultural context of Undset's own era, including biographical material. For a more complete list of work by and about Undset in all languages up to 1963, see Ida Packness, *Sigrid Undset bibliografi* (Norsk Bibliografisk Bibliotek, vol. 22, Oslo: Universitetsforlaget, 1963).

Amadou, Anne-Lisa, "Sigrid Undset satt på spisen." *Spor etter mennesket: Essays til minne om A. H. Winsnes*, eds. Liv Bliksrud and Asbjørn Aarnes (Oslo: H. Aschehoug, 1989), pp. 195–201.

——, "Viga-Ljot og Vigdis," in her *Å gi kjærligheten et språk: Syv studier i Sigrid Undsets forfatterskap* (Oslo: H. Aschehoug, 1994), pp. 23–29.

Anderson, Gidske, *Sigrid Undset, et liv* (Oslo: Gyldendal, 1989).

Beyer, Harald, *A History of Norwegian Literature*, ed. and trans. Einar Haugen (New York: New York University Press and American-Scandinavian Foundation, 1956).

Bliksrud, Liv, *Natur og normer hos Sigrid Undset* (Oslo: H. Aschehoug, 1988).

——, *Sigrid Undset* (Oslo: Gyldendal, 1997).

Brundage, James A., *Law, Sex and Christian Society in Medieval Europe* (Chicago and London: University of Chicago Press, 1987).

Byock, Jesse L., *Feud in the Icelandic Saga* (Berkeley/Los Angeles/London: University of California Press, 1982).

Clover, Carol, "Maiden Warriors and Other Sons," *Journal of English and Germanic Philology*, vol. 85, no. 1 (January 1986), pp. 35–49.

———, "The Politics of Scarcity: Notes on the Sex Ratio in Early Scandinavia," *New Readings on Women in Old English Literature*, eds. Helen Damico and Alexandra Hennessey Olsen (Bloomington: Indiana University Press, 1990), pp. 100–34.

———, "Regardless of Sex: Men, Women and Power in Early Northern Europe," *Speculum*, vol. 68, no. 2 (April 1993), pp. 363–87.

Crichton, Michael, *Eaters of the Dead: The Manuscript of Ibn Fadlan, Relating His Experiences with the Northmen in A.D. 922* (New York: Knopf, 1976).

Deschamps, Nicole, *Sigrid Undset, ou la morale de la passion* (Montreal: Montreal University Press, 1966).

Dijkstra, Bram, *Idols of Perversity: Fantasies of Feminine Evil in Fin de Siècle Culture* (New York: Oxford University Press, 1986).

Falnes, Oscar J., *National Romanticism in Norway* (New York: Columbia University Press, 1933; reprinted, New York: AMS Press, 1968).

Graham-Campbell, James, *The Viking World*, foreword by David M. Wilson (New Haven, Conn., and New York: Ticknor & Fields, 1980).

Hamsun, Knut, "Ærer de unge" (1912), in *Knut Hamsun: Artikler*, ed. Francis Bull (Oslo: Gyldendal, 1939), pp. 72–109.

Haugen, Einar, *Norwegian Word Studies*, vol. I: *On the Vocabularies of Sigrid Undset and Ivar Aasen* (Madison: University of Wisconsin Press, 1942).

Institute for Comparative Research in Human Culture, Oslo, in collaboration with Mortan Nolsøe and W. Edson Richmond, *The Types of Scandinavian Medieval Ballad*, eds. Bengt R. Johnson, Svale Solheim, and Eva Danielson (Oslo/Bergen/Tromsø: Universitetsforlaget, 1978).

Jesch, Judith, *Women in the Viking Age* (Woodbridge, England: Boydell Press, 1991).

Jochens, Jenny, "Consent in Marriage: Old Norse Law, Life, and Literature," *Scandinavian Studies*, vol. 58 (1986), pp. 142–76.

———, *Old Norse Images of Women* (Philadelphia: University of Pennsylvania Press, 1996).

———, *Women in Old Norse Society* (Ithaca and London: Cornell University Press, 1995).

Jones, Gwyn, *A History of the Vikings* (Oxford: Oxford University Press, 1968).

Jorgenson, Theodore, *Norwegian Literature in Medieval and Early Modern Times* (Northfield, Minn.: St. Olaf College Norwegian Institute, 1952; reprinted, Westport, Conn.: Greenwood Press, 1978).

Kalinke, Marianne, *Bridal-Quest Romance in Medieval Iceland*, Islandica XLVI (Ithaca and London: Cornell University Press, 1990).

Krane, Borghild, *Sigrid Undset: Liv og meninger* (Oslo: Gyldendal, 1970).

Larsen, Karen, *A History of Norway* (Princeton, N.J.: Princeton University Press, 1948).

Laxdæla Saga, trans. Magnus Magnusson and Hermann Pålsson (Baltimore: Penguin, 1969).

Liestøl, Aslak, ed., *Osebergfunnet* (Oslo: Universitets Oldsaksamling, 1958).

Miller, William Ian, *Bloodtaking and Peacemaking: Feud, Law, and Society in Saga Iceland* (Chicago: University of Chicago Press, 1990).

Montreal Museum of Fine Arts, *Lost Paradise: Symbolist Europe*, exhibition catalogue (Montreal: Montreal Museum of Fine Arts, 1995).

Naess, Harald, ed., *A History of Norwegian Literature* (Lincoln and London: University of Nebraska Press, 1993).

Njals Saga, trans. Magnus Magnusson and Hermann Pålsson (Baltimore: Penguin, 1960).

Nordau, Max, *Degeneration*, 3rd ed. (New York: D. Appleton & Co., 1895).

Olrik, Axel, *A Book of Danish Ballads*, trans. E. M. Smith-Dampier (New York: American-Scandinavian Foundation, 1939; reprinted, Freeport, N.Y.: Books for Libraries Press, 1968).

Ørjasæter, Tordis, *Menneskenes hjerter: Sigrid Undset, en livshistorie* (Oslo: H. Aschehoug, 1993).

Poertner, Rudolf, *The Vikings: Rise and Fall of the Norse Sea Kings*, trans. Sophie Wilkins (New York: St. Martin's Press, 1975).

The Poetic Edda, trans. Lee M. Hollander, 2nd ed., revised (Austin: University of Texas Press, 1988).

Pulsiano, Phillip J., and Kirsten Wolf, eds. *Medieval Scandinavia: An Encyclopedia* (Hamden, Conn.: Garland Press, 1993).

Sawyer, Birgit and Peter, *Medieval Scandinavia: From Conversion to Reformation, circa 800–1500* (Minneapolis: University of Minnesota Press, 1993).

Scott, Barbara G., "Archeology and National Identity: The Norwegian Example," *Scandinavian Studies*, vol. 68, no. 3 (Summer 1996), pp. 321–42.

Solberg, Olav, *Tekst møter tekst: Kristin Lavransdatter og mellomalderen* (Oslo: H. Aschehoug, 1997).

Solheim, Svale, "Hestekamp," *Kulturhistorisk leksikon for nordisk middelalder*, vol. 6 (22 vols.) (Copenhagen: Rosenkilde & Bagger, 1956), pp. 358–59.

————, *Horse-Fight and Horse-Race in Norse Tradition*, Studia Norvegica Ethnologica & Folkloristica, eds. Olav Bø, Reidar Th. Christiansen, Nils Lid, and Svale Solheim, vol. III, no. 8 (Oslo: H. Aschehoug, 1956).

Steblin-Kamenskij, M. I., *The Saga-Mind* (Odense: Odense University Press, 1973).

Stocking, George, *Victorian Anthropology* (New York: Macmillan, 1987).

Sturlason, Snorri, *Heimskringla: History of the Kings of Norway*, trans. Lee M. Hollander (Austin: University of Texas Press, 1964).

Turville-Petre, E. O. Gabriel, *Myth and Religion in the North: The Religion of Ancient Scandinavia* (New York: Holt-Rinehart-Winston, 1964).

Undset, Sigrid, "Det fjerde bud," *Et kvinnesynspunkt* (1919) (Oslo: H. Aschehoug, 1982).

————, "En bok som blev et vendepunkt i mitt liv," *Artikler og essays om litteratur*, ed. Jan Fr. Daniloff (Oslo: H. Aschehoug, 1986), pp. 300–308.

————, *Fortællingen om Viga-Ljot og Vigdis* (1909), afterword by Liv Bliksrud (Oslo: Den Norsk Bokklubben, 1995).

————, *Kjære Dea*, foreword by Christianne Undset Svarstad (Oslo: J. W. Cappelen, 1979).

————, *Kristin Lavransdatter. I: The Bridal Wreath* (1920), trans. Charles Archer and J. S. Scott; *II: The Mistress of Husaby* (1921) and *III: The Cross* (1922), trans. Charles Archer (New York: Knopf, 1923, 1925, 1927).

————, *Kristin Lavransdatter. I: The Wreath* (1920), trans. Tiina Nunnally (New York: Penguin, 1997).

————, *The Longest Years* (1934), trans. Arthur G. Chater (New York: Knopf, 1935).

————, *The Master of Hestviken* (1925–27), trans. Arthur G. Chater (1928) (New York: Knopf/Plume, 1978).

————, "Om folkeviser," *Artikler og essays om litteratur*, ed. Jan Fr. Daniloff (Oslo: H. Aschehoug, 1986), pp. 232–83.

————, "Omkring Abrahams offer," *Kritikk og tro: Tekster av Sigrid Undset*, ed. Liv Bliksrud (Oslo: St. Olav Forlag, 1982), pp. 91–100.

————, *Saga of Saints*, trans. E. C. Ramsden (New York: Longmans, Green, 1934).

————, ed., introduction, *True and Untrue, and Other Norse Tales* (New York: Knopf, 1945).

————, trans., *Tre sagaer om Islændinger* (Christiania: H. Aschehoug, 1923).

Wilson, David M., *The Viking Achievement: A Comprehensive Survey of the Society and Culture of Medieval Scandinavia* (New York and London: Praeger, 1970).

Winsnes, A. H., *Sigrid Undset: A Study in Christian Realism*, trans. P. G. Foote (London: Sheed & Ward, 1953; reprinted, Westport, Conn.: Greenwood Press, 1970).

Ystad, Vigdis, "Den historiske romanen," *Norsk kvinnelitteraturhistorie*, vol. II, *1900–1945,* ed. Irene Engelstad, Jorunn Hareide, Irene Iversen, Torill Steinfeld, Janneken Øverland (Oslo: Pax, 1989), pp. 100–108.

A NOTE ON THE TEXT

Gunnar's Daughter was originally published as *Fortællingen om Viga-Ljot og Vigdis* (Oslo: Aschehoug, 1909). The English translation by Arthur G. Chater was first published by Alfred A. Knopf in 1936. In this edition minor translation errors have been corrected, and where appropriate, the Dano-Norwegian ø has replaced the Swedish form ö in person and place names. In the Introduction and Notes, variants in the spelling of Norse names (e.g., Trygvesson, Trondheim) have been made consistent with the anglicized forms used by Chater.

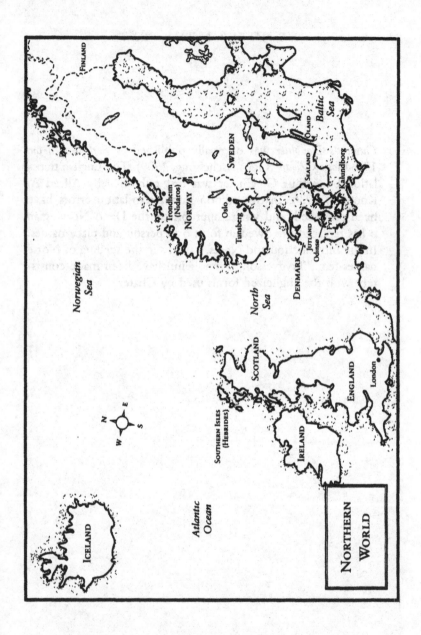

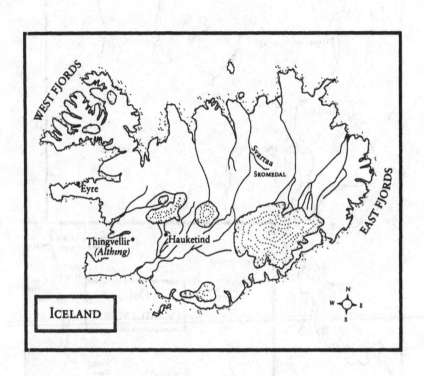

WEST FJORDS

Svartaa
SKOMEDAL

EAST FJORDS

Eyre

Thingvellir
(Althing)

Hauketind

ICELAND

N
W   E
S

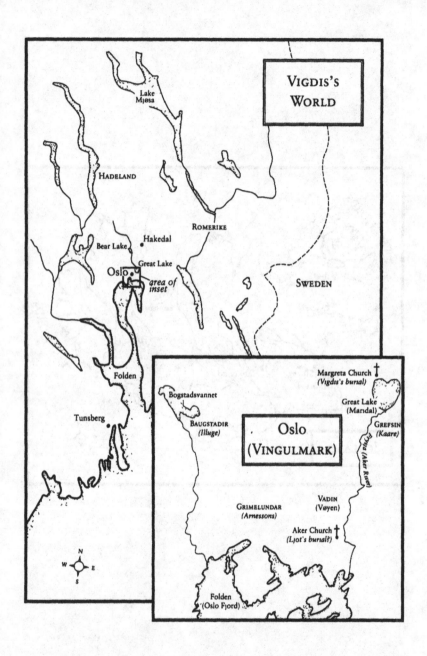

VIGDIS'S WORLD

Lake Mjøsa

HADELAND

ROMERIKE

Hakedal

Bear Lake

Great Lake

Oslo

area of inset

SWEDEN

Folden

Tunsberg

N
W   E
S

Oslo (VINGULMARK)

Bogstadsvannet

Margreta Church
(Vigdis's burial) †

BAUGSTADIR
(Illuge)

Great Lake
(Maridal)

GREFSIN
(Kaare)

Frøya (Aker River)

GRIMELUNDAR
(Arnessons)

VADIN
(Vøyen)

Aker Church
(Ljot's burial?) †

Folden
(Oslo Fjord)

1

Veterlide Glumsson was the name of a man from the East Fjords in Iceland. He sailed often on trading voyages in summer.

His nephew's name was Ljot. He was the son of Gissur Hauksson of Skomedal,[1] who was killed while Ljot was a child. Veterlide took up the suit for Gissur's slaying and bore it with great honour; but that is beside our story. Ljot's mother's name was Steinvor; she died young. Ljot was reared by Torbjørn Haalegg of Eyre;[2] afterwards he dwelt with Veterlide, who loved him as his own son.

Ljot came early to manhood; from his sixteenth year he went a-viking[3] with Torbjørn's sons and quickly won renown for bravery and skill in arms. He was counted a lad of promise and fit for leadership; trusty and loyal, but a man of few words and slow to make friends; he kept to himself for the most part. From certain doings, which are also foreign to our tale, he was called Viga-Ljot.[4]

One summer, when Ljot was twenty years of age, he sailed with Veterlide to Norway. Between them they owned a trading vessel, a fine sea-going ship; Ljot had a third share in her.

2

Veterlide had kinsfolk in Romerike,[1] whom he purposed to visit; he had also to buy building timber in Norway. Summer was far spent when they sailed into Folden.[2]

They rowed the vessel up through the islands, where the river Frysja[3] falls into the fjord, for there was no wind and it had rained all day; but now towards evening the mist cleared and drifted up the hill-sides. Veterlide and Ljot stood in the fore-part of the ship, looking out over the land. It was then covered with thick forest; along the banks of the river were farms, but they were not many and most were small.

Off the mouth of the river some small fishing-boats lay rocking at anchor; the men had their eyes on the great ship which came creeping through the mist among the islands. Veterlide hailed them and asked where they were from. The fishermen, seeing them to be peaceful traders, answered that they were tenants under Gunnar of Vadin,[4] the chief manor on the river here. Veterlide asked whether the fishermen would show them the way thither that evening, and this they promised to do. Then the Icelanders rowed their ship up the river as far as she would float, and one of the fishermen went with them to Vadin.

It was dark when they reached the place. They found Gunnar in his hall, sitting in the high-seat.[5] Gunnar was a big, handsome man with long grey hair and a beard which covered his whole chest. By the hearth sat two women; one of them was spinning by the light of the fire; she was not very young and was darkly clad, but bright and fair of face. The other was but a young maid, who sat with her hands in her lap doing nothing.

2

Veterlide went forward and greeted the master of the house, and before he had told the half of his business Gunnar rose to his feet and bade him welcome, together with his folk, ordering the women to bring food and drink.

They rose at his word, and the elder busied herself; she called to the serving-women and bustled hither and thither; but the younger stood by the fire looking at the strangers. And by its light they now saw that she was very fair, tall and shapely, narrow in the waist, with a high and well-formed bosom; she had large grey eyes, and her hair reached beyond her knees; it was yellow, thick and smooth, but not very bright, and her hands were large, but white and beringed. She wore a garment of rust-red wool, richly embroidered and bedight; her hair was bound with a fillet of gold and she had many rings and jewels, more than women are wont to wear in daily life.

The other woman now came in with a great horn of mead, which she placed in the hands of the younger, saying:

"It is your part, Vigdis, to bid welcome to the house."

She who was called Vigdis then took the horn and passed along the benches, offering it first to Veterlide and after him to all the men. And the last she saw was Ljot.

For at first Ljot had seated himself at the end of the bench nearest the door, but then he had gone forward to the fire, being wet. And he held his cloak about him with one hand; but his black hair came down over his brow, so Vigdis saw little of his face but the eyes, which were dark-blue and deep-set.

When the maiden handed him the horn he dropped his cloak, and as he drank he looked at her over the brim of the vessel; it seemed that she liked not his staring, for she said not a word, but took the horn which he gave her, turned away and went to the raised bench, where she sat down.

Ljot seated himself so that he could see Vigdis. After a while she glanced that way and met his eye; then she looked aside and turned red. But the next moment she looked at him again, and now she returned his stare until he took his eyes off her.

Then a meal was set forth, so sumptuous that it seemed almost a banquet. And Gunnar would have sent his house-carls[6] down to the shore to fetch the ship's folk; he said his men could keep watch by the ship that night.

Veterlide thanked him; but before he had finished speaking Ljot said to his kinsman:

"The hour is already late; our men can surely stay by the ship this night, so that we need not trouble the goodman's carls."

At this Vigdis laughed, saying:

"This Icelander must be very fearful for his goods."

Gunnar reproved her, but without anger; he said:

"It is well bethought of the Icelander to spare our housefolk; but 'twill be little trouble for them, and those men who have rowed all day in this bad weather must need shelter and fresh food. But it sounds ill, daughter, to give such an answer to a guest of the house."

Ljot laughed and answered:

" 'Twas not ill meant, I'll be bound—and the words of so young a maid must not be weighed too nicely."

The other woman also spoke to Vigdis, but very quietly, and Vigdis gave no heed to what she said, but smiled faintly as she sat. —Gunnar then sent men to the shore, and the others ate and drank.

The talk was of the heavy grey weather they had had of late, a great misfortune on sea and land alike, for the corn was now ready for reaping. Gunnar said: "In my youth I too fared abroad in summer, and of all weathers I liked this least, with rain and fog and calms."

Then Ljot answered and sang:

> *"Truth hast thou spoken,*
> *Guest-loving Gunnar!*
> *Dark lay the skies on us,*
> *Ran's daughters[7] dozing;*

Little delight
With them to dally.
Rather the roof
Of friendly thane.

Goddesses golden
Decked the board;
Fairer beings
Saw I never.

Fain would I linger
Late in the night
And with yon fenny-sallow fair one
Chop words of cheer."

The last lines were chanted in a lower tone, and Gunnar, who was already somewhat gone in drink, paid no heed to them; but Veterlide marked them well and began at once to talk to Gunnar about his seafaring. Soon after Vigdis and the women went to her bower.[8]

Later, when the men had gone to rest, Veterlide said to Ljot, who shared the same closed bed:

"I marvel at your conduct, kinsman; it looks ill, when Gunnar has received us hospitably, that you make ditties to his daughter the first evening."

As Ljot made no answer Veterlide went on:

"Never before have I known you a great lover of women —but tonight I could not see that you took your eyes from Vigdis. We have not been so long at sea that the sight of a woman should turn your head."

Ljot still made no answer, but turned his back to him and feigned to be asleep.

3

Next day, when they had broken their fast, Gunnar and Veterlide rode down to the shore; but Ljot lay on the bench and said he was tired. He stood up nevertheless, as soon as the others were gone, for he had in mind to seek out Vigdis and talk with her.

Ljot was still clad in his travelling dress, for his clothes lay in the ship. He wore a long, dark, hooded cloak, fastened at the breast with a costly gilt clasp. Under his cloak he had a black tunic, embroidered in every seam with silver and blue, for Ljot was very fond of show. For this reason he wore good rings on hands and arms, and he was well worthy to be seen: he was tall of stature, broad-shouldered, narrow in the waist as a woman, with shapely limbs. His features were handsome and delicate; only he was dark of hue, with large and prominent pale lips. He had blue eyes and long, dark-brown hair tied with a band of silk.

The day was fine and sunny, and when Ljot came out into the yard he saw Vigdis walking in the meadow north of the houses. He went quickly after and came up with her at the edge of the wood; there he greeted her and asked if she had any errand. Vigdis answered that she had no errand but to walk in the woods and eat berries.

"Then will I go with you," said Ljot; "it is unsafe for you to walk alone; I have heard the bear haunts these thickets."

"I might have brought my body-servant, if I had been afraid," answered Vigdis; "and in any case I am not unarmed." With that she showed him a great knife she carried in her belt.

The handle was bound with coils of gilt wire, and the blade was scored with runes.[1]

Ljot took it in his hand, looked at it and said:

"That is a strange knife, and it is surely very old; where did you get it?"

"It has always been in my family," said Vigdis; "they say that my kinswomen were priestesses at the high place in the grove[2] here; but that is a long time ago, no one knows much about it. Our thralls offer cocks and sheep there; but my father believes in nothing but his own power and strength, nor had my grandfather any other faith, as I have heard."

" 'Tis the same with me," said Ljot, laughing. "Though for that matter I was once baptized a Christian."

"That is a strange faith," replied Vigdis. "He can surely be of little help, the White Christ, for I have been told he could not free himself, but was slain by his enemies in Blaaland."[3]

"I know not what to make of it," said Ljot, "and I scarcely think he can do much. But it so chanced that there was a clean-lived man south in Denmark who helped me and healed an ugly and putrid wound I had got in the leg; he would take no other reward, and so I let him baptize me rather than offend him."

"Ay, you must have travelled far afield," said Vigdis, "—but how was it you did not ride with your kinsman to see your goods brought ashore from the ship? You must have something on board which you have won; why else do they call you Viga-Ljot?"

"Oh, I dare say I have won something, and good enough it is," he said; "but I have always thought that what I meant to win was better still."

"I can well believe it," answered Vigdis. "They say the Icelanders are greedy for goods and lavish of words."

Ljot said:

"I never heard of any man who took no care of his goods. But you are the first who called me niggard."

Vigdis laughed at this and said:

"The speech of so young a maid must not be weighed too nicely."

"I almost think you have taken a spite against me, Vigdis," returned Ljot. "You gave me no kindly look when we met just now."

" 'Tis not our custom either in these parts," she replied, "to let our eyes dwell too much upon strangers."

Ljot laughed as he answered:

"I cannot think that if you bind your hair with gold, Vigdis, it is that you may hide behind your women thralls."

"Why should I not wear gold, if my father gives it me?" asked Vigdis.

And now they had reached the high place. It was in a clearing, and the forest was thick on all sides; about the mound stones had been set up in a ring and in the middle was the stone of sacrifice; but many of the stones had fallen, and over the whole place grew saplings of oak and birch and rowan. Among the rocks were many tall tufts of red flowers, and some of them had gone to seed so that their white down was carried on the wind; it settled on their clothes and hair, and Vigdis shook it out as they walked.

Ljot said to Vigdis, as they were eating berries:

"My uncle thinks of asking Gunnar to give us board here, while we look about for timber. But perhaps you would rather see us depart as quickly as we came? For I believe you like us not?"

"My father must decide for himself what folk he takes into the house," answered Vigdis. "It has never been his custom to ask me. But he lets me be mistress of my own doings."

"So I had thought," said Ljot with a laugh. "I take you to be a headstrong and stubborn maid."

"So they say," she answered. "And you seem to me a bold and forward youth."

"Ay, such is my repute," said Ljot. "But may we say now that you and I are not enemies?"

"We do not look to be so," replied Vigdis. And then they seated themselves on a stone and ate fern roots which Vigdis had dug up. But when they stood up Vigdis forgot her priestess's knife. Ljot picked it up unseen by her and hid it in his bosom. After that they went home, jesting together, and were good friends.

Veterlide bought timber of Gunnar. Gunnar refused to take payment for the Icelanders' board, but bade them stay as long as they pleased; and when Veterlide spoke of going on, Gunnar declared that there was no need to hurry. Ljot thought the same in his own mind, and he sought converse with Vigdis as often as he could.

Veterlide spoke to him of this one day when they were alone, and Ljot then uttered what was in his mind:

"I have a great wish to take Vigdis to wife; I have not found any with whom I should like better to live. She is fairer than most women I have seen, large-minded and witty of tongue— and a richer bride I could scarcely find, since she is Gunnar's only child. And I believe that Gunnar likes me."

"There may yet be a doubt whether he would care for the bargain," said Veterlide, "if you would take her so far from home. But if it be true that Vigdis has set her heart on you, that, I think, will weigh most; for the maiden will certainly decide her marriage for herself.[1] And no doubt you know how she is disposed towards you, for you have been much in her company."

At this Ljot grew thoughtful and said after a while:

"Woman's mind is not easy to unriddle. I have often thought she likes me well; but she is quick to take offence— and sweet speech may cover guile."

"I little think there is guile in Vigdis," replied Veterlide; "but the maid is young, and maybe she is unwilling to subject herself to a husband. For she seems to me very self-willed. My advice is that you pursue this matter gently and with becoming slowness. We will now journey northward and visit our kins-folk, and when we come back it will be seen in what mind she is and whether she has missed you."

"I will not go from here," said Ljot, "until I know what is to be the upshot of this business."

5

The same evening Ljot sought out Vigdis in her bower, as she sat on the bench sewing. She was clad in a richly embroidered blue gown, and her yellow hair hung loose about her, shining in the light of the great fire that burned upon the hearth. On seeing him she laid aside her sewing and rose to meet him; but Ljot came hurriedly forward and sat down beside her on the cushion. Vigdis then said:

"What may be the cause of your seeking me here at this late hour, when my father is from home?"

"I have seen little of you these days," replied Ljot; "and there are many things of which I should like to speak with you."

"But we have talked together every day," Vigdis answered again.

"I have much yet unsaid, Vigdis, and of this I would rather speak with you alone. Now Veterlide said today that I must surely know your mind, whether you like me or not. Many times I have thought that you showed a liking for me, but at other times your words were so strange and your anger was so quickly kindled that it almost seemed you bore me a secret spite."

"Why should I bear a spite against you?" said Vigdis. And now she sat for a while in silence, without looking at Ljot. Then she spoke again:

"Strange, that you should say this to me. For I have often thought, as we sat together, that you were hasty of temper, and many a time I could not tell why we quarrelled, or whether you mocked me. I have passed all my days here in the forest, and few folk come this way; but you have travelled far abroad

and seen many things. 'Tis not untrue that I was often angry
with you."

"I have no skill in talking with women," said Ljot slowly.
"But I have met none whose company I preferred to yours.
Nor any other with whom I would care to live."

To this Vigdis made no answer, and he went on quickly:

"If you agree, I will sue for you with Gunnar and take you
to wife."

Still Vigdis said nothing, but Ljot put his hands around her
neck and kissed her on the lips. And as the maid did not move
he drew her closer and took her on his knees.[1] Then she burst
into tears, freed herself and went to the hearth; there she sat
on a stool and all her hair had fallen about her like a veil, upon
which the fire shone; Ljot thought no man had seen a fairer
sight. He followed her and stood with his hand on the pole of
the smoke-vent, looking at her; then he said:

"Ill it is that I should make you weep, my fair one. But now
let me have your answer."

"Give me a little time," Vigdis begged. "Go up country to
your kinsmen, as was your purpose, and when you return to
your ship lying here, I will give you my answer. I almost think
I would have it as you desire; but that it would take me a great
way from my father and he would be left alone. Moreover it
seems to me that this has come very suddenly."

"Not so suddenly as you think," said Ljot. "I have been
here three weeks already. I know not what powers there be
that rule the fates of men; but the Norns[2] have woven ours
closely together, and this I have known ever since the day we
talked at the high place."

"Now I see by your face that you are angry already," said
Vigdis. "I am young, and it is early yet for me to think of
wedding."

At this Ljot turned to go. "I dare say we are old enough—
but I see now that you do not know your own mind."

Vigdis rose and came after him, saying:

"Yet wait the little while I asked you; I would rather your

suit were not in vain. But as yet it seems I know you but little, and you would take me far from all that is mine."

And now she put her arms about his neck and kissed him. But after that she pushed him out of the door and bade him go.

Vigdis kept to her bower for two days after this. Then it happened that a guest came to the house, Kaare of Grefsin.[1]

This Kaare had just come home from Trondheim,[2] and he had much news to tell of Earl Haakon of Lade,[3] who had lately been slain by Kark his thrall, and of King Olav.[4] Vigdis came into the hall at evening; she took her seat by Kaare and the two conversed as friends.

Kaare was very young, fair-skinned, tall and handsome. Ljot was ill pleased that Vigdis sat drinking with him. He said so to Vigdis, when he chanced to be near her:

"You know well enough how you feel towards Kaare of Grefsin."

"That is a true saying," Vigdis answered. "Kaare and I were brought up together, and it gives me joy to see him again."

But after this Ljot kept an angry eye on Kaare, and whenever Kaare spoke well of a thing that evening, Ljot would cap it at once with something yet more worthy to be praised. At last the talk fell upon horses, and Kaare boasted of his stallion, whose name was Sløngve;[5] Gunnar had bred him and given him to Kaare as a token of friendship.

Ljot replied that he had seen him, for they had lately brought the horses home from the forest for the work of harvest. And he held that the stallion he had bought of the sons of Arne at Grimelundar[6] was better still; his name was Aarvak,[7] and, said Ljot, he did not believe a better beast had been seen in those parts.

"Fine enough to look at," remarked an old man who was sitting near Ljot; "but Kaare's horse drove him off the field both this year and last. But you are ill-advised," he said to Ljot, "to speak well in this house of anything that comes from the sons of Arne."

"How so?" Ljot asked the old man.

"There has been great enmity between Vadin and Grime-lundar, since Eyolv Arneson sued for Vigdis and was turned away," was the answer.

"Of that matter I have never heard a hint," said Ljot, and the old man went on:

"Gunnar would have been willing enough to have Eyolv for a son-in-law, but they say that Vigdis refused him. Nor can anyone be surprised at it, for many an ugly deed is told of the sons of Arne, and then they say there has been friendship between her and Kaare since they were children. But the sons of Arne have often threatened Gunnar since; though 'tis likely they will beware of him; Gunnar may be old, but not yet toothless."

Ljot said no more, but sat wrapped in thought with a watchful eye on Vigdis and Kaare. After a while he went up to Kaare and said:

"There has been a great deal of talk this evening; do you not think with me that it would be sport if we tried our horses together so that everyone could see which was the winner?"[8]

"Gladly," replied Kaare with a laugh; "but it is hardly necessary, seeing that it is known to every man hereabouts."

Vigdis then put in a word:

"You must not mar the horse you have bought so dearly; he may be good enough, though another be better."

To this Ljot answered in great wrath:

"I am not so fearful of hazarding my property as you think —let Kaare show us what his horse can do in a bout. Let us drive the horses together tomorrow, and if Aarvak is not the winner he shall not be carried to Iceland by me."

"Eyolv will scarcely take him back," said Vigdis, laughing.

"I shall not ask him," replied Ljot. "If he loses I shall kill the horse."

And now he drew a gold ring from his arm and flung it into the fire that burned in the middle of the floor, crying:

"You shall not cast it in my teeth, Vigdis, that I am too careful of my goods."

But Vigdis bent forward and snatched the ring out of the fire, handed it to Ljot and said:

"Behaving like a witless fool is as bad."

Then Ljot took the ring and threw it into the crowd of thralls by the door, saying he who caught it was to keep it. There was great uproar among the thralls; the one who first got hold of the ring was struck down, and it looked as though the feast would end in a great scandal. Veterlide dashed up to his kinsman, took him by the arm and rebuked him severely, but Ljot only laughed. And amid all the hubbub that ensued it was agreed at last that Kaare and Ljot should match their horses the next day.

7

Men came from all the country round to watch the horse fight; there were also many women present. The place where the horses were to meet was a meadow near Vadin.

Ljot came first, leading his horse and carrying a staff in his left hand. He was armed with short sword and helmet, and wore a fine scarlet cloak embroidered with gold over his shoulders; he took this off and laid it on a stone; under it he wore a short red tunic. The sons of Arne were there; they greeted Ljot and shook him by the hand.

The stallion was a big animal and fine to look at, a promising beast folk thought him; he neighed loudly to the other horses tethered around the field.

Some time passed before Kaare came, and the sons of Arne declared with many taunts that he must be sorry he had taken up the wager, and Ljot joined in their raillery.

Then Kaare appeared, and Gunnar and Vigdis came with him. Kaare was fully armed and bore a coat of mail; he had a bearskin over his shoulders and carried a spear besides his staff.

As soon as Aarvak saw the other stallion he knew him again and must have recalled their encounter in the forest, for he broke away from Ljot, turned tail and tried to escape out of the ring. This raised a laugh among the folk standing round, but Ljot ran after his horse, seized him by the mane with his left hand and struck him with his staff over shoulders and quarters; his face was red as blood. And now he drove the horse forward without mercy.

Sløngve had the other one down at once, struck out with his fore-hoofs and bit so that Aarvak moaned and again tried

18

to escape. Then Ljot drew his sword from his belt and struck at Aarvak, but slipped on the grass and slit the skin of Sløngve's belly with his sword. But his fall brought him underneath the horses; it was an ugly moment. Vigdis shouted loudly that they must part the horses and Kaare ran forward and made a drive at his with the butt of his spear, so that the animal reared for an instant and released Aarvak; Ljot's horse then struggled to his feet and galloped off to the forest, bleeding and sorely punished. But Sløngve's guts were pouring out of the wound Ljot had given him.

Kaare then said, as he gave Ljot his hand to help him to his feet—for Ljot had been kicked about the head so that the blood ran down into his eyes:

"Never have I seen any man bear himself thus in a horse fight. You shall make good the horse to me."

"Here is your payment," answered Ljot, kicking up a lump of mould with his foot. "You scared the horse with that bearskin you wear, like a troll of the woods."

"You won't scare us, Viga-Ljot," said Kaare, "though you may have killed your men up in Iceland"—and now he turned the spear in his hand, so that the point was towards Ljot.

Ljot still held the sword in his hand, and he cut the spearshaft in two and wounded Kaare in the arm, but only lightly; Kaare then threw away the stump of his spear, drew his sword and set upon Ljot. But at that moment Ljot fell backwards in a swoon and the blood ran out of his mouth; the horses had kicked him badly.

Now Veterlide came up, took Kaare by the shoulder and spoke to him, saying he would make good the horse and the wound and let Kaare fix the price himself.

"I will accept no amends from you, Icelander," answered Kaare; "I see well enough that your kinsman there seeks a quarrel with me."

"I will not have it that we fall into conflict with friends of Gunnar," replied Veterlide; "he has deserved better of us." And he took Kaare aside and talked to him.

But Gunnar had taken his spear and run it through Sløngve's counter.

Koll and Eyolv, the sons of Arne, lifted Ljot to his feet, and he came to his senses after a while. By that time Kaare had left the field with Veterlide. Ljot wiped the blood from his face and looked about for Vigdis. She was crouching by the dead horse and patting him, weeping sorely.

Ljot went up to her, laughing, and asked:

"What say you now to this horse fight, Vigdis?"

Vigdis wept even more and said:

"I will not speak with you."

"Are you afraid that Kaare of Grefsin may fare as did his horse?" asked Ljot.

" 'Tis not Kaare that has brought shame on himself today," said Vigdis. She drew the mane back from the horse's head and stroked his muzzle; "but now I have no more to say to you." She stood up, went to her father, weeping, and left the field with him.

The sons of Arne came over to Ljot and bade him go home with them.

"That I cannot do," Ljot answered. " 'Tis not fitting that I break friendship with Gunnar thus."

"I wonder," said Eyolv, "if Gunnar be not more afraid of losing the friendship of his son-in-law."

"Whom call you so?" said Ljot.

" 'Twill be Kaare no doubt," Koll joined in; "though it cannot be certain that he will pay the price for her, seeing she has already let him have his will."

"That's a lie, sure enough," said Ljot.

"So said I too," replied Eyolv, "when our herdsman came and told us he had seen Kaare ride across the river last spring and meet Vigdis in the grove; he said Kaare lay with her then."

"He lied sure enough, your herdsman," Ljot answeed again, turning to go. But Eyolv asked some who were standing apart: "Which way went Kaare of Grefsin? Viga-Ljot would speak with him."

"Oh, he went to Vadin with that other Icelander," was the answer.

Ljot stood for a while looking towards the manor. He was an ugly sight, pale as a corpse and smeared with blood. Then he turned, and as he did so he nearly fell. The sons of Arne took him by the arms, helped him to mount a horse, and now he rode with them westward to Grimelundar.

8

Veterlide was not too well pleased that Ljot had taken up his abode at Grimelundar; he rode thither some days later and found his kinsman lying in the upper room.

"I am now reconciled to Kaare," said Veterlide, "and I beg that you will not break the peace with him."

Ljot made no answer to this, but asked after a while:

"What do they say at Vadin about this business?"

"Nothing much," replied Veterlide; "as was to be expected of Gunnar, for he is a man of generous mind and it would give me little pleasure to hear what he thinks of your conduct."

Ljot lay silent for some moments, plucking hairs from his coverlet; then he told Veterlide what the sons of Arne reported that their shepherd had seen.

"Much weight there must be in what Eyolv's shepherd says—even if all his sheep say the same," commented Veterlide. " 'Tis the way of jealous old women to spread such stories; an ill thing it is, kinsman, that you take up with fellows like these."

"You might find out how Gunnar is minded towards me in the matter you know of," said Ljot after a while.

"It is a bad time to ask such questions, while you lie here," answered Veterlide. "I would rather you went back to Vadin with me now."

"I have a pain in my back," said Ljot; "I am not fit to ride."

"If you could ride one way you can surely ride back," said Veterlide. " 'Tis not surprising that you do not relish a return to Vadin, for you have won little honour in this business, but you will have to do so; that is my advice. The sons of Arne are planning to put enmity between you and Gunnar; they are afraid to set on him alone and they would push you before

them—but let them sit and spin their sheep's wool by their
own hearth and do you leave their schemes alone."

But Ljot stood out that he was not fit to ride. The sons of
Arne invited Veterlide to stay for food and drink; but he would
not and rode back to Vadin at once.

It turned out as Veterlide had said; when he spoke to Gunnar
about Ljot, saying his kinsman had set his heart on Vigdis,
Gunnar answered:

"Unwilling I am that there should be unfriendliness between
us, Icelander, for I think highly of you, and I would gladly
believe Ljot Gissurson to be better than his conduct here would
show; but I have no desire to send my daughter with him over
the sea, nor to fetch my son-in-law from Grimelundar."

"None can wonder at that," replied Veterlide. No more was
said of that matter; and no word reached Vigdis of their talk.

9

Veterlide spoke several times to Ljot, trying to get him away from Grimelundar; but each time Ljot said he was very ill; he spat blood and had pains in his head. He declared he could not accompany Veterlide on his journey to Romerike, and when Veterlide returned thence and was ready to sail home to Iceland, Ljot wished to stay behind in Norway. At that the other was also unwilling to leave, "for," said he, "if you stay here with the sons of Arne they will surely tempt you to some deed that will bring shame on you."

"Go with an easy mind, kinsman," Ljot answered. "I am now well enough to make my way northward to Romerike, and afterwards I have a mind to seek King Olav and meet the men from home who are at his court.[1]—And the sons of Arne have not asked any help of me, but merely shown me friendship."

"Do you promise me to go northward?" asked Veterlide. Ljot gave him the promise, and when he had left the neighbourhood, Veterlide sailed for Iceland. He parted from Gunnar in a most friendly fashion and they gave each other rich gifts; to Vigdis he gave a golden brooch and a mirror of Southern workmanship; she bestowed on him at parting an embroidered cloak of red silk.

10

Autumn was well advanced when it was rumoured in the district that Viga-Ljot had come back. He dwelt with a man named Torbjørr at Hestløkken,[1] in the forest between Grimelundar and Vadin; but he was often in company with the sons of Arne.

One evening a little boy came to Vadin and asked if he might speak with Vigdis. His name was Helge and he was the son of a poor woman who lived in the forest not far from the manor. He said his mother lay sick, and would Vigdis of her charity go with him and see if she could help the woman. Vigdis answered that Æsa—such was the name of her foster-mother, who had charge of the household at Vadin—was the better leech; it would be more to the purpose if she went. But the boy held to it that his mother would rather speak with Vigdis; she had something to say to her. Vigdis then put on a cloak and went with Helge.

It was dark when they came out. They followed the road at first, but then the boy turned off towards the edge of the woods; he said the fields were too wet for them to cross, for it was the last day of October. As soon as they entered the forest, where a cattle-track ran, a man came towards them. Vigdis asked who he was.

"It is I," replied the man; "Ljot."

Helge then tried to withdraw his hand and run away, but Vigdis held him fast and asked him:

"Was it this man that sent you after me?"

The boy did not answer, but Ljot said:

"I did so; he was going to fetch Æsa, and then I bade him make it so that I had speech with you; for I guessed it would avail me little to seek you at Vadin if I was to speak with you alone."

"You choose a strange way of seeking me," Vigdis protested.

"Well, I knew no other," said Ljot. "I have tramped here long enough around the manor waiting for a chance of meeting you."

Again the boy tried to run from them, but Vigdis held him by the hand; then Ljot begged her:

"Let the lad go; I suppose you are not afraid to be here with me, and I shall take you home to the houses."

"Go then," said Vigdis to Helge, and then turned to Ljot: "What have you to say to me, since you had to lure me thus into the forest?"

"You know very well what I have to say to you," was Ljot's answer.

Vigdis made no reply, and Ljot went on:

"I know now that the longer I stay away from you, the more I yearn for you, and the day will never come when you pass out of my mind."

Vigdis began to weep as she answered:

"Then why have you fallen out with my father?"

"Chance so willed it," said Ljot. "They are saying hereabouts that Kaare of Grefsin is to wed you."

"Do you think I would then have received you as I did, that evening you spoke to me in my bower?" said Vigdis. "But the first thing you did was to spoil everything for us."

"Yes, that was bad enough," Ljot answered. "But in this matter of Kaare 'twill be for your father to decide, I'm thinking."

"Gunnar shall never bring it about that I take any man but of my own choosing—and that he has promised me," said Vigdis.

"Then will you take me?" asked Ljot, and Vigdis answered: "Yes, I will, if it can be brought about."

"Ah, then it will be strange indeed if it be not brought

about," said Ljot in great gladness, taking her in his arms. He sat down on the root of a tree with her on his knees; she put her arm around his neck and kissed him. But then Ljot would not let her go and kissed her so hotly that she was afraid and said she must go home.

"It will be best I go down with you, then I can find your father this evening; I am minded to have this matter settled with goodman Gunnar quickly."

"Do not so," Vigdis begged him; "you are alone, and you have no other weapon than that spear."

Ljot laughed and said: "Well, is not that enough, think you?—but 'twill be a bad day's work if it should come to blows between Gunnar and me."

Vigdis reflected for a moment and then said:

"I have heard it said there are many Icelanders with the King in the North; do you know any of these men?"

"I do indeed," replied Ljot. "There are Toralv and Gissur Torbjørnsson; they are sons of my foster-father."

"Can you not go up and speak with them?" asked Vigdis. "If they would be your spokesmen it would make the matter easier with my father."

"You have some haste to have me hunted from these parts," said Ljot, and he took her on his knee again. Vigdis then began to weep, saying:

"I fear it will go amiss if you bring forward this suit alone, seeing how unruly you are, and now Gunnar is angered against you. It were far better you had someone with you who could give you support and counsel."

Ljot pushed her off his knee, and she began to walk homewards, weeping all the time. Ljot followed a pace behind. After a while he said:

"I shall do as you say, Vigdis—though you know 'tis a long journey with winter coming on. Nor is it certain that the Torbjørnssons will be so eager to come south with me. What shall I do then?"

"Well, then you must act for yourself," said Vigdis, and now

she turned and took him by the hand. They walked together
down towards Vadin. Ljot promised her that he would go
north, and would leave on the morrow. They parted at the
gate, but before he went Ljot said he would meet her once
more. He took all her hair in both hands and wound it around
his neck and hands:

"You must come up to the high place tomorrow, for I have
had no sight of you all this time, and this evening it was dark
—but I shall be there before sunset—and then there is a thing
you lost, last time we met there, and you shall have it back. I
have taken care of it; I thought it would furnish an excuse to
see you, if such were needed."

"I know not what it may be," said Vigdis. Ljot laughed and
said she should see. And so they parted.

11

When Vigdis came in it was so late that all had gone to bed. She went straight to her bower, and Æsa brought her milk and bread. While Vigdis ate and drank, Æsa asked how it was with Astrid.

"You must go and see her tomorrow," said Vigdis, and after a pause: "I did not get so far this evening."

"How then, did you lose your way?" asked Æsa.

"Not that either," replied Vigdis, and was silent a few moments; but then she said: "I met Ljot out in the fields here and talked with him."

At this a woman spoke, who was there washing up pots and pans—her name was Torbjørg and she was married to the headservant at the manor:

"Now I never heard the like; is that Ljot hanging about the place?—then I warrant he means mischief."

"Oh, 'tis not so bad as that, I'm sure," said Vigdis with a laugh.

"Beware of him, Vigdis," the woman went on, and now she came up to the bench; "soon he'll be saying he has seduced you, he too."

Æsa bade her be quiet—"but have no more to do with Viga-Ljot; none can tell what may come of such things."

"Why, the girl is no longer a child, since she is past eighteen," said Torbjørg. "Better for her to hear it, so she may beware. 'Twould be an ill thing if folk were such fools as to believe it—he has made songs while he lay in these parts, and they are all about Vigdis. And Ljot it is who spread the tale that Kaare has debauched Vigdis—though 'tis clear to all he

29

acts as do little children, when they besmirch what is out of
their reach."

"Ljot never said that," Æsa put in. "That tale was set going
by the sons of Arne; it is they who carry slander round the
countryside."

Vigdis sat on the bench, and she went red and white by
turns as they talked. "I'll never believe that Ljot has said a word
about me," she said.

Then sang Torbjørg:

> *"Tenderly toying*
> *I fondled her hair,*
> *As I sat by the fair one*
> *In her father's hall.*
>
> *We two alone—*
> *All still was the house.*
> *Longest will linger*
> *That night in my heart.*

—But I never heard that Eyolv Arneson was a scald,"[1] she said.
Vigdis made no answer; and Torbjørg went on:

> *"Silent they sat,*
> *Great birds of the forest—*
> *Late was the season,*
> *Summer had flown.*
> *Bright red berries*
> *She brought me to feast on.*
> *Better that sport*
> *Than the spoils of fowling."*

"Now I have heard songs enough for this evening," said
Vigdis. She went and lay down. Æsa shared her bed; she was

well aware that Vigdis had little sleep that night; but Vigdis lay still and said nothing.

Next day Vigdis came before Gunnar and took a seat by him. She asked:

"What answer would you give Ljot Gissurson, Veterlide's kinsman, if he came here and sued for your daughter?"

"Let him first come here to my house," replied Gunnar; "then I shall give him an answer that he will remember. But he will beware of showing himself now."

"But that matter between him and Kaare has been settled," said Vigdis.

"Veterlide has made his peace with Kaare," answered Gunnar, "but not Ljot. No man has rewarded my friendship more basely."

"He cannot have known what has happened between Eyolv and us," said Vigdis.

"Well, now he knows full well what has happened," replied Gunnar, "and much which has not happened. But now we purpose, Kaare and I, to seek him out at Hestløkken. And I shall hack the teeth out of his jaw, then we shall see what ballads he can be making."

"That shall never be—" said Vigdis in great fear. But Gunnar commanded:

"It shall not be that you speak with him again, and I will hear no more of him from you."

Vigdis said nothing, but went out.

12

The whole of that day she sat in her bower sunk in great dread and bewilderment, not knowing whether to go and meet Ljot or not. But when it was drawing on towards sundown she wrapped a dark cloak about her and went out into the yard.

There had been a frost the night before and the mist lay white over the fjord; the sun stood due south over the hills shining brightly. There was no one in the yard; Vigdis stood hesitating for a moment, but then she left the manor hurriedly and went northwards to the forest; no one saw her go.

When she reached the high place Ljot was there already. He was dressed for the journey, but had put off his cloak and arms and had tied his horse to a tree. He ran to meet Vigdis, shading his eyes with his hand, as he said:

"Now it seems the sun would grudge me a sight of your beauty—welcome hither, Vigdis."

He put his hands on her hips and turned her away from the light; but she tore herself from him and put her arms behind her, saying:

"Hither am I come; but I have strange questions to ask you—tell me now, is it true that there has been talk in the neighbourhood about Kaare and me?"

Ljot answered—and he turned very red as he did so:

"That is what I asked you yesterday—if it were true he was to wed you."

"Now I would I had not come," said Vigdis. "For now I fear they spoke the truth whom I thought to be lying."

"I know not what you mean," said Ljot.

Then said Vigdis:

"Either you have talked of that which has passed between

us—and never had I thought you would have breathed a word of it to any mother's son—or it is you who have made up the ditties that are going about."

Ljot kept silence. Seeing this Vigdis turned and would have left him. He followed her, saying:

"The truth is, I wish those ditties had never been made. But you know not how sick at heart I was all that time, when I thought I had lost you. At such a time many a man will say things that he afterwards regrets."

"Ah, and now I regret most of what I ever said to you," Vigdis answered.

"Speak not so," Ljot begged. "You shall never again have cause to reproach me."

"I know that," replied Vigdis; "for this is the last time you and I will talk together."

Ljot put his arm round her; she tried to push him away, but then he caught both her wrists and said:

"It cannot be as bad as that, if I have made a song or two —you cannot have loved me much if you would leave me on that account."

"You cannot have loved me so much either," said Vigdis in great wrath; "no sooner did you hear evil spoken of me than you believed it and spread it abroad."

"No tale have I spread abroad," he answered; "and never did I believe it."

"It may come true for all that," she said, trying to wriggle out of his embrace.

"I'll not hear you say such things," cried Ljot, and he kissed her. "You must have forgotten what you promised when you sat on my knees yesterday."

At that she bit him in the neck, so that her face was hidden from him for an instant.

"Now my mind is changed," she said.

"Never shall Kaare sway your mind," said Ljot between his teeth. "I do not care to live if I am to lose you." And then he took her in his arms and lifted her up, in spite of her struggles.

He carried her into the grove, and there he had his will of her, though she resisted for a long time. Afterwards Vigdis said nothing, nor did she weep at all; Ljot felt her hand and cheek. She was very cold.

Ljot rose to his feet, took his cloak and covered her with it; he kissed her. It had now turned so cold that his breath hung in the air as a white mist; the sun had gone down, but the sky was red as blood in the south behind the trees.

"It is time to be going from here," said Ljot, trying to raise her to her feet. "We can go no farther than the Great Lake tonight; there we shall find some place where we can shelter."

Then said Vigdis:

"It were far too good a death for you, dastard that you are, if my father came after you and cut you down."

She got up and walked towards home; Ljot followed her, saying:

"It were best for us both that you came with me—I know I have offended you sorely; but the greatest misfortune that could befall us would be to lose each other."

Vigdis did not once turn round, and that she neither spoke nor wept seemed to Ljot the worst sign that could be. He followed her all the way to Vadin.

When they reached the fence Vigdis bent down; she picked up a stone and threw it at Ljot.

"Be off with you, dog," she said.

The stone caught him on the mouth, not hard, but enough to draw blood. Then he said:

"Once more shall I woo you, my playfellow, but first you shall have time to reflect—when summer comes I shall ask you again if you will have me."

"Then you shall see, Viga-Ljot, that my will is as strong as yours."

After that she went in. She went straight to her bower and to bed; Æsa was well aware that she slept but little that night and moaned in her sleep; but she said not a word of what had befallen her.

Ljot went back to the high place, untethered his horse and rode away. He travelled all night and reached Hakedal[1] by morning; from there he made for Romerike and then rode straight to Trondheim without heeding the bad weather which had just set in; he suffered great hardships in crossing the mountains, so that his foster-brothers, the sons of Torbjørn, thought it a marvel that he had come through alive.

13

Vigdis now sat at home at Vadin and was so full of sorrow that nothing could cheer her; she hardly cared to take food or drink, to dress herself or comb her hair; never could she take her thoughts from the wrong Viga-Ljot had done her. Every night she dreaded going to bed with these thoughts for company; but towards morning she dreaded rising again to face the long day to be spent in working and chatting with others. She said to herself:

"Now I am like a bird that lies on the ground fluttering its broken wings; it cannot move from the spot where it has fallen, and it cannot see farther than the stream of its own blood. If I think upon what used to be, I remember only what is now. If I recall the time when I lived here blithe and carefree, it seems it was only that this might come upon me." Often she thought it would be best if she went and lay down in the river. Winter was now on the wane; then she found she was with child.

One night when she lay awake, while Æsa and the other women slept, she got up, put on a cloak and went out into the yard; she took the downward path leading to the river.

Vigdis had never before been out at night alone, and it seemed to her more dismal than she had thought possible. It was the time of the equinox, with much wind and rain, so dark that she could not distinguish earth from sky; but now and again there was a rift in the clouds and stars came out. She had not gone far before she felt she had strayed from the path into the fields, but could not see where she set her foot; at times she waded through drifts of melting snow, or one foot would plunge down into a hole, but for the most she found a slippery frozen surface, for the snow had been washed off the ground where it sloped down to the Frysja. After a little while she could not tell where she was, or where was the river and where the manor. Vadin lay close to the stream, but in the darkness it seemed an endless journey. At last she slipped on the frozen ground and slid down till she came up against something and threw her arms around it; she guessed it to be a fir-tree, as the branches scratched her face. But as she slid down she could feel that the child moved within her.

Vigdis crouched under the tree; she was as wet and cold as if she had been lying in the snow. She crept closer in, so as to have some shelter from the rain; but the wind howled and crashed in the tree-tops around her and the darkness was full of ugly noises; she did not know what things were prowling and shrieking round about her.

She lay there till the first light of dawn; then she saw that just below where she lay was a steep drop to the river; the water was dark as pitch and full of drifting ice. Her courage was now quite gone and she walked back to the manor; it was not far, now that day was dawning. She undressed and lay down in her bed, and so wretched was her state that she thought some mortal sickness would follow her night's wandering, and that would be best.

In the morning Æsa asked:

"How is it your clothes are so wet, foster-daughter?"

Vigdis answered that she had been out to the byre during the night—there was sickness among the cattle that year—"and it was so dark that I could hardly find my way back to the house."

Æsa asked no more, but merely remarked that Vigdis should have spoken to her.

One day Æsa said that Vigdis must be sick, her look was so changed and she sat drooping on the bench. And she begged her earnestly to confide in her foster-mother. But Vigdis answered that she was not to trouble herself about this.

Gunnar was ailing that winter, so that not many folk came to the house; and as the season wore on Æsa contrived that there were no other women at Vadin but herself and Vigdis. Vigdis fashioned herself a laced garment that she wore under her dress, and for the most part she stayed within doors; thus it was that no one noticed her state, except Æsa; but she dared say nothing.

14

When spring came Vigdis said that this summer she would live at the sæter[1] with Æsa. And so it was agreed, though Gunnar was against it; but Æsa at length talked him over. They then left for the forest very early in the season, taking with them a man whose name was Skofte. He was Æsa's son and a freedman[2] of Gunnar. He was to tend the horses and guard the cattle from wild beasts.

One day towards evening Æsa stood at the door of the byre letting in the cows; when Vigdis came up to her in great distress and said:

"Here is Gunnar coming up the hillside—I know not what will happen—he will surely kill me when he sees how I am now."

"Go to your bed," replied Æsa; "I will tell him you are sick—he will not stay long."

Vigdis did so, and kept her bed the two days Gunnar was there. He said it was not to be wondered at that she had fallen sick, or that they were short of milk, seeing how early they had gone to the hills—while the nights were still frosty and there was little pasture in the woods.

But after this Æsa made up her mind that she ought to speak to Vigdis and give her some advice; so she said one day, as the other stood at the bench scouring milk-pails:

"Let me do that; you must not work so hard now."

Vigdis flung her pail to the ground, and her eyes were so wild that they frightened her foster-mother; she screamed aloud:

"Not a word of that to me, or I know not what I may do to you!"

After that Æsa never dared to speak of the matter to Vigdis.
And now summer was wearing on.

One night Vigdis got up and left the sæter. It was past midsummer, the weather was calm and cloudy. She walked some
way over the paddock; when she came to the fence she could
do no more, but had to lie down and wait awhile. A dun horse
was grazing at the edge of the wood; he did not keep with the
rest, but stayed near the houses; he was much petted and spe-
cially fond of Vigdis. He came now and sniffed at her, stood
over her as she lay there. When the pangs abated a little she
stood up and walked along the cattle-track; the horse followed
her the whole time. Each time the pains came on she threw
her arms about his neck and leaned against him, and then he
turned his head, nibbled at her shoulder and back and stood
quite still.

At last she reached a large, dark sheet of water. High up
there was a break in the clouds, reflected in the tarn; all else
was black and dismal. Once she shrieked loudly, but the echo
from the crag on the other side of the lake was so horrible that
she was afraid of being heard and stuffed a corner of her cloak
into her mouth. She bit it into little pieces, filling her mouth
with shreds of wool, and thought they must choke her. She
heard a running brook close at hand, and once, on opening
her eyes, she saw that dawn was breaking; little black wavelets
ruffled the tarn, but she could not crawl down to it, and the
time wore on miserably for her.

The sun came up and began to hurt her eyes. Not long after
Vigdis was delivered; then she lay for a long time in a swoon,
but at last she felt the sun warming her and she heard the child
scream. She looked at it; it was a boy. She shrank from touch-
ing it, but took a kerchief she had worn over her head and
shoulders; it was white with green stripes, damp with sweat and
dew and stained with blood. She folded it about the child,
pushed it in between two stones and spread moss and twigs
over it. Then she made her way to the brook and drank.

There was a great bare rock by the side of the water; the

sun had warmed it and Vigdis leaned her back against it, resting there awhile. Then she got up and dragged herself home to the sæter.

There she found Æsa in great distress. Skofte had gone out to search for her. Vigdis went in and lay down on her bed; she had fever and was very sick for some days. Æsa took care of her and rubbed her breasts with warm butter; but neither of them spoke of what had happened.

Vigdis would never again go out into the forest, but stayed within doors. Æsa could see no sign that she was less sorrowful than before.

15

Late in the summer the weather grew very warm; the cows did not come home at evening, but lay out in the forest; Æsa and Skofte had to make long search over hill and bog to find them and bring them in.

Vigdis was loath to be left alone at the sæter; she had a dread of the forest and was impatient to go home. She sat most of the day on the threshold looking out. The sæter stood high, with hills and forest on every side; but she had a glimpse of the cultivated land and the fjord in the south. She was sitting there listlessly one evening, when the dog who lay with his nose in her lap grew restless; he started up and dashed down the meadow barking, and then Vigdis caught sight of a man dismounting and tying his horse to the fence. She was alarmed and rose to her feet, meaning to make for the wood and hide; but at that moment the man turned, and she knew him for Ljot. He called out, bidding her not to be afraid.

Vigdis stood still in the doorway, and answered:

"I know well that I have no need to be afraid of you."

Ljot halted and looked at her for a moment; then he asked slowly:

"What do you mean by that?"

Then Vigdis gave an ugly laugh, but made no answer.

Ljot stood leaning against the door-post; he looked at the ground and turned up mould with the point of his spear as he spoke to her:

"I am now bound for home; there is a ship lying at Tunsberg,[1] owned by my kinsmen. I know very well that it is a great boon I ask of you—that you shall forgive me all the wrong I have done you. But so it is, that if you will now go with me, you shall have more honour and greater love than has been given to any woman before you."

Vigdis laughed again and answered:

"Your promises are of little worth, Ljot. You lured me to you once with fair words, and then you brought on me the direst shame and sorrow past bearing—no woman has suffered worse. Great honour indeed would be hers whom you took to wife—'tis great honour to pick quarrels, to kill folks' horses and debauch maidens and make up lies and ballads. And you look to be fit for no other deeds of daring, you ghastly bugbear."

Ljot looked away as he answered:

"It is true that you have good cause to say this to me. But I have performed other and better deeds in the past—and you were once ready to hear of them. Then I did not look to you so ugly that you were not fain to kiss me again and again. But I have had little gladness since we last spoke together. And bitterly have I longed to meet you again."

"Maybe you thought," asked Vigdis, "that I sat here waiting to see you again?"

Then Ljot looked up in her face and said: "Yes."

After that neither of them uttered a word for a while. Then he asked again:

"Tell me now, Vigdis, whether it be true that I have a child in these parts or not?"

Vigdis laughed and answered:

"That may well be—but I know nothing of it. I have not inquired of your dealings."

Ljot turned red as fire and held his peace. Vigdis said:

"Now go and make ballads of your manhood and boast of how bold a fellow you are when you are alone with a woman. But do not expect them to believe you hereabouts—no one here takes much account of a jealous suitor's gossiping."

Ljot stood silent, not knowing what more to say nor finding it in his heart to leave her; he saw clearly that she would not change her mind, and that there was small chance of his ever

finding her again. And it seemed a grievous thing to lose her.
Then he called to mind the priestess's knife; he took it from
his bosom and handed it to her, saying:

"Do you remember that you dropped this last year, the first
time we were at the high place together?"

Vigdis took the knife, and with a sudden movement she bent
forward and struck at his throat. The blow caught his collar-
bone, ripping his clothes and tearing the skin so that the blood
flowed. Then Ljot seized her and drew her to him for a moment. He said:

"Now, Vigdis, I could take you with me—but now I will
not act against your will. But come with me—and whatever
harm you do me I will repay with good."

Vigdis answered in his arms:

"You shall not get me alive over the water."

He kissed her and said:

"Then I wish that much joy may be yours—but I shall never
forget my sorrow."

Vigdis answered:

"May you have the worst of deaths—and live long and
miserably—you and all you hold dear. And may you see your
children die most wretchedly before your eyes."

Ljot released her and went down across the meadow. He
untied his horse. But then he turned and stood for a while
looking up towards the sæter. After that he led his horse into
the forest and rode on. And many years passed and much happened ere he saw Vigdis again.

16

They came home from the sæter in late autumn. That winter again Vigdis was only moderately well. And she was greatly disquieted when Kaare of Grefsin and his kinsmen began to treat with Gunnar, that he should marry her to Kaare. Vigdis begged that the matter might stand over for a time, saying she was unwilling to be married so young. In the end Gunnar promised Kaare an answer by autumn, but Vigdis saw that her father had set his mind on this marriage.

Vigdis said she would not dwell at the sæter that summer. One evening in spring she walked out over the meadows; it was towards sunset and fine weather, just at the time when the birches come into leaf and the birds are singing; there was a pleasant smell of leaves and grass, and Vigdis thought she would walk and try to forget her sorrow.

South of the manor dwelt a woman in a little hut; she was married to one of Gunnar's house-carls. She sat on the threshold spinning on a distaff as Vigdis went past, and Vigdis stopped and spoke to her. There was a child crying inside the hut. Vigdis said:

"That child cries as though it were in great sorrow—it cannot be very young. For I have noticed that new-born babes scream so horridly—more like a cat or an owl than any human sound."

The woman went in and took the child on her arm; it was a little girl, of two years or more. She was quiet again as soon as her mother had her, and after a while she crawled down and ran about plucking flowers. She was still so small that when she bent down she tripped over her frock and fell. Vigdis picked her up, and then the child gave her the flowers she had in her hand; but she had plucked them without stalks, so Vigdis dropped them at once. Then her mother said:

"These flowers are called night-and-day;[1] take one, Vigdis, and give it to me, then I will tell your fortune."

Vigdis did so, and the other said:

"It has first two dark petals and then two light; but I see the lowest petal is light at the centre and dark at the edge. That means that at first you will have great sorrows, but afterwards much joy. That dark edge to the last petal is a bad sign, it betokens no good for your old age."

Vigdis answered:

"That is a bad prophecy, methinks, and I have not asked you to tell my fortune either. But I must reward you nevertheless." With that she took a little filigree brooch from her bosom and gave it to the woman. Then she went on.

There was a slab of rock out in the meadow; around it grew some rowan-trees and briars, and the grass below was full of night-and-day. When Vigdis reached it she sat down, clasped her knee in her hands and looked out over the fjord, which lay shining grandly in the south, now that the sun had gone behind the hills. She stayed sitting thus for a long time—and little comfort had she in her thoughts, whether she remembered Ljot, or called to mind that which she had hidden up in the forest. She had often wondered whether it lay there yet, or whether it was wholly devoured. She remembered clearly that in the place where she had lain that night were many ants and other foul creeping things, and although she had little kindness for the child she had borne, it seemed a horrid thought that the ants might have crawled over it before it was dead.

She rose up when darkness was coming on, and walked homewards so quickly that she almost ran. On coming near the manor she met Æsa, who said:

"You gave me such a horrid fright, foster-daughter; I did not know what to think when you stayed out so long, you who are so afraid of the dark."

Vigdis answered:

"Afraid of the dark I am now, and of the forest, and afraid at home in my own bower. Wretched is my life, and better were it for me to make an end of it."

"Do not say such dreadful things," said Æsa; "all may yet be well with you. You are young enough to forget your wrongs—and for aught anyone knows you are a maiden pure. Kaare loves you, and with him you will have an easy and honourable lot."

"*That* now seems to me the worst of all," replied Vigdis; "I think it were better that my shame were made known openly —even if my father drove me out of his house. There is nothing worse than to be forced to jest and seem merry as I used to be, when I can never turn my mind from the misery that has befallen me. And it is no great help to me if they believe me hereabouts to be a pure and undefiled maid, when there are three of us who know it is not so. I bear the secret mark of it on my body—I know not how to save myself, now that Kaare has begun to press his suit."

That evening, as they sat alone in the bower, Vigdis took this up again, and said to Æsa:

"Might you not have a mind, foster-mother, to go south to your kinsfolk among the sounds—you have often said they were of no meaner birth than our kin here?"

Æsa answered:

"I know not whether my kinsfolk be alive or dead, and now it is too late for me to seek them out or change my condition. But why do you ask of this?"

Vigdis was silent a long time, but at last she said:

"In old days, whenever I was sorrowful, I would go to you and sit in your lap. But now it has come about that I am more secret with you, Æsa, than with any other."

Æsa made no answer, and the other spoke again:

"I now regret that I set out that child, for every night it wakes me with such horrid screaming. But evil fortune should harden my heart, as I would have it."

"What mean you by that?" asked Æsa.

"It were my best revenge," replied Vigdis, "if Ljot's son became Ljot's slayer. Not lightly would he escape from the dog I reared with hate and blows, till he had his teeth in Viga-Ljot's throat."

Then Æsa said in a very low voice:

"Now I would fain know whether you mean that."

"I do so," replied Vigdis, and her foster-mother went on:

"Then it is best I tell you that the boy you bore last summer is with Skofte, my son."

Vigdis rose from the bench on which she sat; she stood for a moment speechless and pale as a corpse. Then she flung herself down and wept with her head on the table.

Æsa said:

"None need get to know of it, and my advice is that it be kept hidden as before; but I have told you, in case you desire to see your son."

But Vigdis lay lamenting and said:

"I thought I was already so unhappy that my life could not be made worse. But now I can no longer bear to live in these parts, when I know that boy is here and my eyes may light upon him—'twas bad luck I was so tired and wretched I had not the strength to throw him into the lake. I do not believe you have told me the truth."

Then Æsa went to her chest, took out a linen cloth and handed it to Vigdis. She looked at it—it was the same she had had on that night; it still bore the stains of blood, and moss and mould clung in the folds. She flung it on the floor and said, weeping:

"Now my father will know all—I will not live if I have to beg Skofte or any other to keep my secret. Never did I think you would fail me so badly."

Æsa answered:

"When I awoke that morning and you were not in your bed I was frightened and bade Skofte search for you. He found the boy and picked him up; we thought him so handsome a child that Skofte offered to rear him. But I have told you this because I thought it might console you somewhat to hear you had the fairest child alive."

"Well, now it must turn out as it may," said Vigdis. "For I am weary of this life."

Æsa answered:

"You must not do this. Honourable birth is of little avail—she who has to bear a shame will be brought low. That has been my fate, as I shall tell you; afterwards you must make your choice."

17

Æsa then told her story:

"My father's name was Harald Goldbeard and he dwelt
south in Sealand;[1] often have I told you of my childhood, how
bright and happy was the life we led, I and my sisters. They
were fully grown, Ingrid and Astrid, but I was thirteen, when
one evening we went with our serving-maids down to the
sound and bathed. Some ships came sailing past; they were
vikings from Öland.[2] They landed and took us on board; not
one of us was able to escape. Three brothers owned the ships
and they took us three sisters for themselves; they saw at once
which of the maids were of gentle birth. Arngrim was the name
of the eldest; I lay with him the first night, and after that he
had me for two years. The brothers soon parted; the others
made for home, but Arngrim roamed over the sea winter and
summer; he was a brave, strong man and a handsome, but he
treated me harshly, because I would never show him affection.
My sisters I have never seen since, nor heard what became of
them, for Arngrim would not answer me when I asked for
news of them.

He sailed far and wide and won many victories. He kept me
in a room below the deck; fearing I might escape he took my
clothes from me, but gave me great store of costly skins and
coverlets and jewels. There was a Danish lad on board whose
name was Asbjørn; I enticed him to fly with me, taking all the
gold, but Arngrim got to know of it; he slew Asbjørn, and after
that he treated me worse.

One time, as we lay under the Southern Isles,[3] some vikings
from Norway laid their ship alongside, and then Arngrim fell.
Gunnar, your father, was their chief. When he led me out of

the cabin I went to where Arngrim lay dead on the deck; I knelt down and washed my hair in the blood that flowed from him, remembering how Arngrim used to tie my hair about his neck at night. Never had I a more grateful washing.

Then Gunnar asked me my name and of what kindred I was; for, said he, I can see you are as well-born as you are beautiful. After that we talked together that day and that night. Gunnar promised to carry me home to Denmark; he gave me the best of clothes, suited to my station, and showed me such kindness that he won my affection; he said he wished he were parted from his wife, then he would accept me at the hands of my kinsmen. But I would rather stay with him than go home; I was with him in his ship till I was with child; then he loved me even more, for Alvsol was childless.

He brought me hither to Vadin; but then the Earl summoned the thanes to arms, and Gunnar had to leave me. He bade Alvsol take good care of me and of the child, as though it were her own. Then we parted, and I was left behind with unspeakable sorrow and longing. Alvsol and her foster-mother were with me when I gave birth to a son; they took the child from me at once and had it set out, but forced all the household to tell Gunnar it was stillborn, and Alvsol promised me the cruellest of deaths if I made complaint. Afterwards tidings came that Gunnar was sorely wounded and could not be expected home for a long time; then Alvsol had me taken to the house where her thralls lived. One of them was named Svart; he defended me against the rest, and was good to me in other ways, but he took me to wife; Alvsol gave him a house here in the forest, where Skofte now lives, and she let it be known to all that now I was the wife of the thrall.

When Gunnar came home she told him that I had gone to Svart, and at this Gunnar was so angry that he was about to kill us both. But I told him about the boy she had exposed, and all the rest. Then he drove Alvsol out of the house and bade me leave Svart and come and rule his house. But I advised him rather to take a new wife; so he married Herdis, your mother, and she was younger and handsomer than I was then. As you know, she died when you were born; then I asked Gunnar to let me have the nurturing of you, and this he granted. Since then I have had charge of the house, as you have seen, and Gunnar cared well for my sons and gave them their freedom—in all things he has acted by me for the best, so long as I have known him."

18

Vigdis said:

"Of all you have told me it seems most strange that you stayed with the thrall in whose power they placed you—I should have begged Gunnar to have him torn asunder by wild horses."

Æsa answered:

"It was more honourable for Gunnar to take a rich and high-born wife than to keep me in his house. But what swayed me most was that I had Svart's child—I would not have them take my son from me a second time."

"Your nature is not as mine, foster-mother," said Vigdis. After a moment she went on: " 'Twas no great joy he had of my mother either—and still less will it be when he hears I have this child."

"Let the boy bide where he is, while Gunnar is alive," said Æsa. "Afterwards you can take him to you and find comfort in him. We shall find some way to deal with Kaare."

Vigdis folded her hands in her lap and looked down into the fire. "I have no heart to go on living in sorrow and dread, trying to hit upon a way," she said; "rather will I take the worst that may come, and it can hardly be worse than what I have to bear now."

She took up the wrapping, went to the door and called to a man who was chopping wood in the yard.

"Take this cloth to Skofte," she ordered, "and tell him he is to come hither this night and give me back that which he found with the kerchief."

After that she went back and seated herself by the hearth. Æsa sat opposite. For a long time they did not speak; then said Æsa:

"It will be late ere Skofte can be here. It were best we went to bed."

"Go then and lie down," replied Vigdis.

Æsa said nothing and did not move. After a while Vigdis said again:

"Go you to bed now, Æsa."

Her foster-mother could hear by her voice that it was in-advisable to thwart her, so she went and lay down, but she did not sleep. Vigdis stayed up; she did not move, except to put wood on the fire whenever it was dying down. And so the night wore away, till the cocks began to crow.

After a time there was a knock at the door.

"Go, Æsa, and open," Vigdis ordered.

Æsa did so, and Skofte came in. He carried the boy on his arm, wrapped in a pelt. Vigdis rose, took a torch of pine and lighted it. Skofte uncovered the child and held it to the light, when it began to scream, for it had slept till now.

Vigdis looked at the boy for a moment, but did not touch him. He was small and thin for his age, with long dark hair and light blue eyes. He was very like Ljot.

Skofte put him down on the floor, for he wanted to show that the boy could already stand on his feet, if one held him —but he could not walk. He cried the whole time and clung to his foster-father's clothes.

Vigdis threw the torch upon the hearth and sat down as before. Skofte said, as the boy would not keep quiet:

"He cries because he is sleepy—in other ways he is as good as can be."

"Then lay him down," replied Vigdis; "or he will wake the whole house."

Æsa took him in her arm and was carrying him to the bed, when Vigdis said:

"I will not have him there—you must find another place for him. And you, Skofte, are to go to the hall and lie down. I shall reward you for this, more than that boy is worth."

Æsa laid the child on the bench and herself beside him. Vigdis remained sitting up all night.

19

Æsa Haraldsdatter[1] went to Gunnar in the morning, while he lay in bed; she ordered the house-folk out and sat down on his bed; they talked together in private a long time. Then he got up, dressed himself and went to Vigdis in her bower.

Vigdis stood up as soon as her father came in, very pale and in great fear. But Gunnar said little, and Æsa stayed near him the whole time. He went over and looked at the child, saying:

"It is plain to see who is his father."

Vigdis made no answer, and then Gunnar spoke:

"Often have I thought it hard that I had only the one child and no sons. But in my belief I always showed you affection and never harshness—thinking I should see you happy and honoured before I died. But I had better been childless than hear you called wanton and see your bastards grow up in this house in my old age."

Vigdis answered:

"True it is, father, that it were better you had no daughter."

Gunnar said no more, but went out.

20

Time went on, and now it was quiet at Vadin; they kept few servants about the manor and little was seen in the neighbourhood of Gunnar and his house-folk. Gunnar took this matter greatly to heart, so that he aged rapidly and became bent and feeble.

The boy was settled there; Æsa looked after him and was fond of him; but Vigdis showed him no affection, nor had she given him any name. She was still sorrowful and went nowhere outside the courtyard of Vadin.

One day Vigdis and Æsa were in the kitchen-house baking, and the boy ran to and fro; he was then two years old. Æsa made two little loaves and showed him how she would bake them for him. This made him so happy that he could not control himself, but danced about the women asking for his loaves, and so he came to upset the meal-bin. Vigdis picked the boy up, shook him and beat him:

"You never do aught but mischief," she said.

The child howled and cried, till Vigdis carried him to the bench.

"Sit there," she said, "and keep quiet; I will not hear you weep for so little."

She went back to her kneading-trough and busied herself for a time with her bread. Then she said to Æsa:

"Not much joy shall I have of this child, and I scarce think he will be the bane of any man. He does not take after me; I did not weep when he was made—but perhaps his father was not far from it."

"You must not talk like this," replied Æsa.

Vigdis said no more and turned to her work again. The boy

could not check his tears; but he held his hands before his face, and when his mother looked at him he lay down and buried his head in some sacks that lay on the bench.

After a while Æsa went out. Vigdis then took the little loaves from the griddle, went across and gave them to the boy.

"Be quiet now and eat these," she said and laid them in his lap. The boy stopped crying and looked at his mother; he fingered the loaves, but found them too hot, and he was afraid. Seeing this she stroked his hair two or three times. But after that she told him to go out to Æsa.

21

That winter wore on and nothing happened that is worth relating.

It was past the equinox and the sun was gaining power down in the valleys, so that the snow on the roofs thawed in the daytime. Folk were felling timber in their woods, and one morning Gunnar rode out with one man to see to his house-carls, who were at work west in the forest.

About midday Æsa and Vigdis were in the hall setting food on the table, and Æsa looked out of the door.

"Gunnar is coming home already," she said; "—but he seems to sit his horse strangely—he must be either drunk or sick." With that she went out to meet him. Vigdis took the porridge-pot from the fire and was setting out spoons, when she heard a great cry from Æsa. And now they came in, Skofte and another man, leading Gunnar between them; Æsa walked beside them wringing her hands. Vigdis then saw that her father's face was pale and that his white beard lay bloody upon his chest.

Vigdis dropped all she had in her hands; she ran to her father and asked what had happened.

Gunnar made signs that they were to carry him to the bench; he sat for a while leaning his head against the wall, then he said:

"This has happened: I have spoken with Eyolv of Grimelundar, and our speech took such a turn that we shall have no more words together."

Vigdis asked quickly:

"Is Eyolv killed?"

"No," answered Gunnar; "but doubtless my end is at hand."

Æsa and Vigdis undressed Gunnar and looked at his wounds; they saw then that he spoke the truth. Vigdis said:

"Now you must tell us, father, how this came about."

Gunnar answered:

"It so chanced that we met in the woods, Eyolv and I, and he used words to me about you, Vigdis. You can guess I did not keep calm and let him throw my daughter's dishonour in my teeth."

Vigdis made no answer. They laid Gunnar in his bed. He bade Skofte go north at once and bring his house-carls home to the manor, for there was no knowing what the sons of Arne might do now, and, said he, "Eyolv swore he would make Vigdis his leman."[1]

Æsa seated herself by Gunnar, but Vigdis took Olav, the man who had been with Gunnar, into a corner and questioned him closely.

"How did you defend your master, Olav?"

"As well as I could," the man replied. "And Gunnar defended himself as you would expect of him; we killed each a man, but there were six of them. When Gunnar got his death-blow I ran to him and caught him as he fell from his horse, and then the others rode off."

"Do you know whither they were heading?" asked Vigdis again.

"I know that the Grimelundings are lying by the tarn nearest the Gautestad wood, that they call the Child's Tarn," replied the house-carl. "They are felling timber on the ridge there."

Vigdis was silent for a moment. Then she said:

"I dare say Eyolv thinks he did a good work before his dinner. 'Tis likely the swine sleeps now, with a full belly."

After saying this she went out and crossed to the bower. She opened her chest and took out the priestess's knife, bound a dark kerchief about her head and put on a black cloak. Stepping into the courtyard she found skis and staff in the penthouse, and now she set out on skis across the fields up to the forest and kept along the edge of the woods towards Gautestad. She

turned north of the houses and followed the low ridge that
runs behind the manor. There was a hard crust under the trees
and her skis ran lightly, so it was not long before she sighted
the white plain around the tarn and the log-cabin that the
Grimelundar folk had there.

There were signs that many men had passed over the ground
and timber had been drawn there; it covered with chips
and bark and wisps of hay. But there was no one to be seen.
Vigdis kept among the trees and stole under cover up to the
cabin. She slipped off her skis and peeped in.

An axe and a shield lay by the door, and she knew them for
Eyolv's. The cabin was three logs high and very narrow; she
entered and saw that two men lay there asleep. One of them
was Eyolv.

Vigdis went first to the other sleeping-bench; she took the
cloak that the man had spread over him and wrapped it about
his head; with her other hand she drew the knife and thrust it
into his throat. The man died at once. Then she turned to
where Eyolv lay.

Vigdis put her hand on his breast and woke him:

"Awake now, Eyolv—you are to get what you long have
sought for; here is Vigdis from Vadin to make sport with you."

Eyolv started up from his sleep; the cabin was dark and he
could not see her clearly. Vigdis said again:

"True it is that I have lost my honour, since I have come
to you in your bed."

As she spoke she struck at him with the knife. And this time
Vigdis did not miss her aim; Eyolv fell backwards and the blood
gushed from his throat. She plunged the knife into him twice
again, and the last time she did not draw it out, but let go of
the haft and leaned forward to watch him die.—She drew her
hands through the blood that poured from him and dried them
in his hair. And when Eyolv had breathed his last, Vigdis went
out, put on her skis and started off through the forest.

It had turned colder, and Vigdis moved rapidly, for now the
way was mostly downhill. But now and again she had to stop,

as her legs trembled under her, and all the time she could see Eyolv dying under her hand. And it was to her as though she had now taken vengeance for more than Gunnar's death; she had now done violence upon a man, and he was no more able to defend himself against her than she against Ljot. The thought stirred her so intensely that she did not know how wildly she ran on and scarcely saw where she was going.

And so it chanced, as she was mounting a slope, that she came into a logging-track, and there she met Koll Arneson and some of his men; they were driving empty timber-sledges, and they saw her and called to her. Koll and another man ran out into the snow after her; but the crust was not hard enough to bear them and they had no skis. Vigdis turned off through the copsewood towards a stream that ran below and took to the ice, though it was grey and water-logged—it barely held her and broke behind her skis; but over she came, and so she got away from them.

After this she did not stop till she reached the yard at home, and then she went straight into the hall and up to Gunnar's bed. He was asleep, and Æsa sat beside him. Vigdis cried out:

"Wake up, father, I have welcome news for you—I have now done what I could to lessen our shame, for Eyolv Arneson is killed by me."

Gunnar bade them raise him up in his bed, while Vigdis told him of her doings. Then Gunnar asked her to bend down that he might kiss her; he said:

"You have now shown yourself a brave and manly woman —as I once hoped you would prove. And I no longer harbour anger against you for letting that Icelander seduce you. But I wish you all well, you and your child."

Vigdis then told him of her meeting with Koll, and Gunnar asked if he had recognized her.

"That I cannot say," answered Vigdis. "But he will recognize the priestess's knife—and that I left with Eyolv."

To this said Gunnar:

"Little power have I to protect you, and it may be long ere

Skofte comes back with the men. It will be best for you to take the boy and go to Grefsin at once; I can trust Kaare that he will not forget the good I have done him. But Olav is to take all my goods here and hide them in that pool in the river, south of the hill on which our outer barn stands."

"I will not leave you now, father," said Vigdis, but Gunnar replied:

"It is my wish that you save yourself and your child, for I will not see our race perish—there is little strength left in me; I have lived long enough. But go you at once to Grefsin, you and Æsa."

Æsa said:

"I am no good for running on skis—and I will not leave you now, Gunnar; good master that you have been to me and mine. Nor is it certain that Koll will come for us here to-night—but Vigdis must go, and Kaare will surely give us all the help he can."

Thus it was settled, that Æsa would stay with Gunnar; they could not dissuade her from it. Vigdis went to her bower, woke the boy and dressed him. She collected her most costly possessions, gold and jewels, in a leather bag and put some bread and smoked meat with them, for there was no time to feed the boy before they left. Then she took him on her arm, went back to her father and bade him farewell. Gunnar kissed them both. Afterwards she took leave of Æsa with great affection and prayed they might meet again.

22

She then went out and put on her skis, binding them fast to her feet with thongs. She had chosen a staff with a long iron spike and a ring. She tied the boy firmly on her back with a kerchief and went rapidly out of the yard northward.

The sun was now going down and the crust was so hard that her skis scarcely left a mark in the snow, though she was carrying the boy on her back. She made for the river and followed its course upstream till she found a place where the ice was safe. Then she went on up the slopes, where it was heavy going; she was tired too after her journey earlier in the day. When she had gained the high ground she stopped and looked back; the sky was now red over the fjord; there was no sign of life as far as her eyes could reach—but at that time there was much forest and copse-wood over the countryside.

Vigdis went up towards Grefsin; she did not move fast and the stars were coming out before she reached the houses. There was no light to be seen when she entered the yard, and all the doors were closed. Vigdis went up and knocked with her ski-staff, but no one came out and there was not a living sound except that of the cows moving in the byre. She saw then that no one was at home.

While she stood thinking what was to be done, she put the boy down to get her breath. As she did so he plucked at her cloak and pointed to the south. Vigdis looked that way. And now she saw a red glare in the sky where Vadin should be; it grew larger and larger and with it was a cloud of black smoke. —The boy was afraid and began to whimper, hiding his head in her lap. Then she lifted him up, saying:

"Now they are burning your grandfather and Æsa, your foster-mother—look well, boy, that you may never forget it."

She could see now how the fire was spreading; the flames shot up, colouring the smoke red and golden; the barn had caught, hay and corn whirled up into the sky in sparks, and it became as light as day, even where Vigdis stood. Then she saw many men on skis running quickly across the fields towards the river, and she thought it unwise to stay longer and best to make for the forest.

Vigdis took the boy up again and went as quickly as her skis would run. She thought it best to follow the tracks leading from the house for some distance, so that any who might come after her would not pick up her trail so easily. And she made for the northward, for she knew there were folk living by the Great Lake[1] beyond the valley, and she thought they would not search for her so far as that.

It was dark when she came into the forest and she went by the light of the snow among the trees. The way was uphill and it was bad going, so that she fell forwards many times and cut her face and hands so that the blood flowed. The night was cold; but she had no feeling of it, for the sweat poured off her and her heart was beating so that she almost thought it would burst; worse than that, the boy hung on her neck, and as she went uphill he nearly strangled her.

At long last she found she was at the top of the ridge and it was easier going—but it looked almost as though no one had passed this way before. When she turned round Vigdis still saw the glare in the south between the tree-tops, but it was now much paler.

After a while the boy began to whimper again; he was cold and hungry.

"Do not weep, little one," said his mother. "Soon we shall come to some dwelling; then you shall have porridge and be put to bed."

"Shall we soon be there?" asked the boy.

"Yes, now we shall soon be there," said Vigdis.

She unfastened her cloak, wound it about the child so that he lay as in a bag, and tied him tightly on her back. She now saw a white glade running downhill; using her staff as a brake she zigzagged down the slope, but the ground was rough and every time her skis were brought to a halt she felt her knees shaking and the sweat poured off her. The night was now starry, but it was hideously dark in the forest, for the moon would not rise till towards morning.

At last she saw a white plain below her and guessed it must be the lake. She found a way down and started on it, but ran against a tree and fell, and then she felt that the binding of her left ski had broken. She had a knife on her and cut some withes and mended it as well as she could, setting the boy down in the snow the while.

It was some time before she was ready to go on; then she asked the boy, as she lifted him up:

"Are you cold, my son?"

"No," said he. She felt his hands, and they were like ice; he felt nothing when she pinched them, and she guessed they were frost-bitten. Then she set him on her lap and rubbed him with snow, till it hurt him and he began to cry. She wrapped him round as well as she could and set out over the lake towards the north-west, for there she knew the houses lay.

She then felt she had been chilled while tending the boy. And there was a keen wind from the northward over the lake; Vigdis had the wind against her and it bit through her sweat-drenched clothes, making her feel almost naked. She kept under the western bank, looking out for a house, but saw none. At last, on a white slope, she saw what she took to be a house; she went up and found it was an outlying barn. Vigdis was then so worn out that she could go no farther. She found the door, and it was open; so she got her skis off and went in. It was pitch-dark in the barn and no warmer inside than out; but she felt with her hands till she found some hay in a corner. She buried herself in it, but the hay was cold as ice and did not give much warmth.

The boy asked if they had got there and if he was to have porridge.

"They are not at home, the people of the house," said Vigdis. "You are tired, I know—but we must lie down and go to sleep; they will soon be here."

"I am so hungry," said the little boy. She then took out of her bag a little bread and meat, chewed it and put it in his mouth. He was quieter after that; but he was shivering with cold, and so was she. Then Vigdis unfastened her clothes in front and took the boy against her bare body, wrapped her cloak well about them both and stacked up the hay as well as she could. The boy fell asleep, and it warmed her a little to have him there breathing against her bosom; she slept a little between whiles, but started up, thinking she was wading through snow in the darkness—this woke the child, and she prattled to him, as women do with little children.

After that they lay a long time, and she heard the walls cracking in the frost. Through a crevice she saw that the moon was now shining on the snow; the boy woke again and was thirsty. She was thirsty too, and thought she would go out and fetch snow and find if she was able to move for the frost in her limbs. He was crying and would not let go of her; she had him on her arm as she went to the door.

"Now they are coming home, the people who live here," said the child. Vigdis saw then that there were men on the lake far to the south; they carried torches. She went out and put on her skis again; and when she had gone a little way she thought it better than lying in the barn. But she began to wonder how this journey would end; she had now come to a river and was following its course. She had heard there was a river running into the lake from Hakedal, and she thought she must follow it, if she had the strength, till she came to some dwelling; but she did not know how far it might be. And the farther she went the wearier she grew, and now it seemed that in the end she would have to lie down under a pine-tree with the boy and move no more—nor did she think that any great loss. But still she went on and on; she crossed a great, long lake and had the wind dead against her again—then far away she heard the howling of wolves and quickened her pace, thinking perhaps it was so cold that the wolves would not get wind of her.

At last she could hear the wolves no longer, but only the sound of the river below the hillside on which she was going, and the moon shone bright and cold, and the shadows lay long and black upon the snow. Then she saw a great dark patch under the trees, and she was at the end of her strength. She crept in, broke off spruce twigs, as many as she could, and drew her legs up under her, took the boy in her lap and wrapped her cloak around them both, to keep him as warm as she could. She rested her chin on his head, and then she knew no more, but slept and dozed as she sat there holding him.

23

As day was dawning Vigdis saw that she was sitting on a lofty ridge; above her the mountain rose straight up into the sky, and below her ran a rapid river in a narrow valley. The boy was asleep and did not seem to have taken any hurt. Vigdis thought she must try to find the way to some dwelling—but she did not know where she was, and she was so weary and heavy-hearted that she did not move.

After a while she tried nevertheless to rise to her feet; but as soon as she moved there was a clang close at hand, and an arrow flew out between the trees and buried itself in the trunk of the spruce under which she was sitting. And while it was still quivering a man on skis appeared where it had come from. He halted on seeing her, and his surprise was so great that he stood speechless for a moment before asking:

"Is anyone here?"

Vigdis had not the strength to answer; then he came up to her, and on seeing the child in her arms he was even more astonished. He was a big man with long, fair curly hair and beard, clothed all in skins, with an axe at his belt, a bow over his shoulder and a spear in his hand.

He spoke to her and asked how she had come thus far; but Vigdis merely sat looking at him and could make no answer. Then the boy said:

"They have burnt down grandfather's house."

"When was that?" asked the man; "and where stood that house?"

"I am from Vadin," said Vigdis. "It was this night."

"Have you come so far this night?" said the other. "That was the worst journey I ever heard of for a woman."

After a while he said again:

"You must be got under a roof—'tis but a poor house I have, but better than here."

He lifted her up, put his arm around her and was going to carry the boy; but the child held fast to his mother and would not go to the strange man, and so Vigdis said she could carry him herself. The man then put his arm around her and helped her down towards the river. After a while, when he found she could scarcely stand upright, he took off her skis, and then he carried both Vigdis and the boy and her skis a long way, and she knew little more until they came to a narrow mountain track; it led to a little hut, and there he set her down. He said then:

"It has gone badly with that hand of yours," and he lifted up her left hand; Vigdis then saw that it was greenish white and clear, like ice. He then drew off her socks and shoes and rubbed her with snow a long while; but that left hand still had an ugly look. At last he gave it up and led her into the hut to a bed; he gave her a drink from a horn and she fell asleep at once, though her hand pained her.

Late in the evening Vigdis awoke, and now she saw that a fire was burning on the hearth and around it sat three men, ill-clad in rags, but well armed and bejewelled. They were the one she had met in the forest and two more.

The pain in her hand increased, so that she was scarcely able to eat of the food the men offered her. And it grew worse and worse as the night wore on; her whole arm was aching and it spread to her breast.

In the morning the man she had first met—his name was Illuge—asked how she felt. Vigdis answered that she had never known such pain, and asked if he thought it might mend.

The man looked at her hand and thought it had an ugly look. Vigdis said:

"Then you must help me and cut off these three fingers."

Illuge looked at her for a while, but judged at last that she was right. And so it was done; one of his companions took her

in his arms and held her so that she could not move, and Illuge
took off the three middle fingers of her left hand. Vigdis made
no moan, but merely said when it was done:

"You are a strong man, Illuge, and deft-handed, I should
judge."

Illuge then bound up the wound and put her to bed. She
was ill for a time, but after that she began to mend and was
able to tell the men all about her journey.

24

These three men who lived in the hut were outlaws; Vigdis well remembered having heard of such fellows, who were said to make these forests unsafe for travellers. Two of them were brothers, named Ille Hermod and Einar Hadelænding. Illuge, the third, had come from the north country.

He was a very handsome man, tall and well built with small hands and feet, good features, a hooked nose, blue eyes and long, curly fair hair and beard.

One morning, when Vigdis was much better, Illuge came in to her as she sat alone with the boy. They talked together for a while; then he said:

"We have been talking, my companions and I—it is not easy for us to get ourselves a woman up here in the forest. Your case is not much better than ours, since you are driven away from the haunts of men. Now this is what we must do: you and I shall share a bed, and when spring comes I shall build a house for myself farther north on the lake. Hermod and Einar will also see to getting themselves wives."

Vigdis sat with the boy on her lap; she answered:

"I have too good a trust in you, Illuge, to think you will force me."

Illuge answered after a pause:

"Force you I will not—but I do not know why you should wait; for in the end you must take one of us, and I think I have most right to you. There is a good place here for fishing and hunting by the lake which we call Bear Lake.[1] And you will be better off, you and your boy, than you could have looked to be when I found you."

Vigdis answered:

"You must be content with much less than one would expect of men like you, if you will live in a miserable clearing in the depths of the forest far from any dwelling—I cannot see why you and the others do not come back among your fellowmen. I do not believe any man would dare to deny you peace where I come from, for there is none that can compare with any one of you."

Illuge told her it was not so easy to leave the forest as she thought.

Vigdis said:

"I am not minded to let Koll Arneson, who burned my father in his house, drive me and my son from our home—though I am but a lonely woman and young too. I know well where father hid his gold before he died, and I mean to get that back too. But if you will help me, you and your friends, I will share with you, as is the custom among comrades, and our fate shall be alike."

"You are a bold woman," replied Illuge; "but Oslo lies too near and our deeds are too well known there. If King Olav were not in Hadeland² this winter, it might be."

Then said Vigdis:

"It may be that is best of all for us. I have good cause to appeal to the king—and I have heard too that he preaches the new faith and is very friendly towards all who will become Christian. But at my home there are many who hold fast to the gods and sacrifice at Thor's temple—my counsel is that I go to King Olav, and if none of you dare go with me, it will be well enough if one show me the way through the forest. Then I think our lot will be better—and I promise it shall be the same for you as for me."

After this Vigdis had more talk with the outlaws about her plan. Einar Hadelænding, who was the youngest of them, greatly wished to try to win back his father's estate, and Hermod said he had long been tired of this rough life; his heart was set on getting a ship and leaving the country. Illuge was less ready to yield and often talked with Vigdis when they were alone, saying she must be his wife. Her answer was that they might talk of that when she had got back Vadin. And in the end Illuge promised to accompany her northward to the king in Hadeland.

25

Vigdis and Illuge came to the king's house on the day King
Olav and his bodyguard were keeping Palm Sunday. They
were given shelter in a house near by.

After nones they went to the king's lodging, and Vigdis
asked to be brought before King Olav. She had made herself
as tidy as she could, and she came forward with a courtly and
handsome demeanour and stated her case well. The king kept
his eyes on her while she was speaking, and when she had
finished he said:

"You have suffered a great wrong, Vigdis, if these things are
as you say—and I have heard of these sons of Arne before, that
they were evildoers. But who is your companion?"

Illuge then stepped forward and said:

"They call me Illuge the fair, lord, and these last years I have
been living in the forest south of here."

At this the king frowned and answered:

"I have heard your name before—perhaps it had been better
if it were not so; and better for your cause, Vigdis, if you had
had other spokesmen than outlawed robbers and bandits."

"The matter is thus, my lord king," said Vigdis; "these men
helped me and saved the lives of me and my son when I was
driven from my home like a bitch. And Illuge showed me the
way hither when I asked him—although he is an outlaw and
risked his life in doing it. Therefore, my lord, it is not fitting
that I accept any help of you until you give me a promise that
he shall have protection and safe-conduct home to his forest,
if you will not grant that he make his peace with you."

The king then said that Illuge should have immunity while

the Easter festival lasted, and that they would discuss these affairs later. He bade them be his guests till all things were settled, and in the days which followed he had much talk with Vigdis and she had to tell him the whole story of the slaying of Eyolv Arneson and of her doings since.

On Easter Eve he sent for her; he was alone in the hall and he bade her sit on the bench beside him. It was late in the evening. He now asked her about Illuge, and whether he was the father of her child. Vigdis answered no, and said there was nothing between her and Illuge in that way.

King Olav then asked whose was the boy, and where was he, and why she was not married.

"I know little about him, my lord," said Vigdis; "he was not of this country. I was young and foolish, and so I let him seduce me—but I do not like to speak of him, and I beg you, ask me no more of this."

The king put his arm around her and said:

"You are not likely to stay long a widow, Vigdis, seeing you are so fair and wise."

Vigdis tried to rise, but King Olav held her and set her on his knees. Then she said:

"My life has not been such that I wish to love again. But now I beg you, my lord, to let me go, for the hour is late."

King Olav laughed and kissed her, saying:

"Rather will I have you stay with me—do you not think, Vigdis, we are well suited, you and I? And it were no shame for you to be my leman. I would reward you well for your love."

"This does not become you, my lord king," replied Vigdis. "You can have any maid you will, and need not drink of the cup another has tasted before."

The king laughed yet more and kissed her again, saying:

"Your lips taste just as sweet for that, Vigdis."

And now he picked her up, laid her on the bench and would sport with her.

Then Vigdis pressed her hand against his breast and said:

"Greater sorrows did he bear for you, that god in whom you believe, than will be yours if you let me go my way."

King Olav released her. After a moment he rose and said she might go if she wished. Vigdis put her feet to the floor. She now felt less unwilling to stay with Olav than before. But the king remained seated on the bench and did not speak to her. So after a while she rose and went out of the hall, over to the women's house.

Now came the two great holy days, and while they lasted the king did not speak to Vigdis. But on the third day he sent for her again. There were then many of his men with him.

He now said he would send men with her to Grefsin and would help her cause, so that she might be righted in every way. He also promised to help Illuge and his fellows to make their peace. But after saying this he went aside with Vigdis, and now he fixed his eyes on her as he asked:

"Tell me truly, Vigdis—will you be married to Illuge the fair when you get back your manor?"

Vigdis looked up and answered him:

"You think far too meanly of me, my lord, if you believe I would rather play with the wolf than with the lion. But now, since I see you have shown me such great kindness that I am well assured there is none like you among chieftains, I have another boon to ask: let a priest go with me to Vadin and grant that I may be taught and baptized in your faith. For this I see—my father put all his trust in his own strength, and I too once held the same belief—but now I understand that your faith is the best."

King Olav then softened and was pleased with this. Illuge was also baptized, and he stayed with the king, as did Einar Hadelænding, when their causes had been settled; but Hermod bought himself a ship and left the country.

The king sent some of his men south with Vigdis, a priest among them. They went to Grefsin, and Kaare received her well. She now heard that on the night Vadin was burnt they had been at a banquet, all those from Grefsin. When Kaare saw the fire he collected men and set out after Koll Arneson; when they met Kaare killed Koll. After that they had made a long search for Vigdis, but found no trace; they then thought she had perished.

The matter was then brought to judgment at the Thing,[1] and no compensation was awarded for the sons of Arne; but those who represented them had to make reparation for the killing of Æsa and for the damage done to houses and cattle at Vadin, and the fine was a great one.

Vigdis had the houses rebuilt in the summer; she throve greatly and was soon held in much repute for her courage and husbandry. She had her son baptized and called him Ulvar,[2] because she had carried him that night through the wolves' forest. Afterwards she caused a church to be built of good timber on the hill to the southward by the river Frysja.

Folk in the Oslo country accepted the new faith and Vigdis was steadfast in her baptism; though she was not very zealous in the faith, for she had much to see to on her estate. And now many years passed and all was quiet at Vadin.

But now the tale must return to Ljot.

26

Torbjørn Haalegg of Eyre has been named before; it was he
who fostered Ljot Gissurson. He was a wealthy chief of good
repute. Torbjørn had many sons by his wife, but they do not
concern this tale. The eldest was called Lyting; he was now
dead. Lyting's widow was named Gudrun; she was called the
Sun of the East Fjords, for she was reckoned among the fairest
women of Iceland; and she was very rich, a wise and capable
woman, good and loyal to her friends and kind to the folk of
her household, but hot-tempered, self-willed and not a little
proud. Lyting and Gudrun had but one child, a daughter,
whose name was Leikny.[1] Folk said she took after her mother,
but only in what was good, and Leikny Lytingsdatter was well
liked by all. But Lyting had given her a promise that she should
never be married against her will, and many men had sued for
Leikny, but all had been given a nay.

Ljot came home to Iceland the same autumn in which he
had spoken with Vigdis at the sæter. The first news he heard
was that Veterlide was betrothed to Gudrun, and their wedding
was to be held six weeks after mid-winter. Ljot went straight
to his home, Skomedal, and there he stayed the whole winter,
seeing no one; he did not come to his kinsman's wedding, and
there were many who wondered at that.

In the summer, when men repaired to the Althing,[2] Ljot
stayed at home. Veterlide and Gudrun were at the Thing, and
on their way home they came by Skomedal. They showed no
anger with Ljot for not coming to their wedding, but pressed
him so much to go with them to Holtar that at last he joined
them, though for a long time he refused.

Veterlide now made a great feast, and many folk came to it.

The banquet was sumptuous and all went handsomely, but many remarked that Ljot seemed sad and cheerless; he spoke little and would not join in the sports.

One of the first days of the feast Veterlide wore a splendid embroidered cloak; it was the one that had been given him by Vigdis. Ljot looked long at that cloak. Late in the day Veterlide had laid it aside on the bench; Ljot then took his seat beside it, picked it up and spread it over his knee. When Veterlide came back Ljot said:

"Make an exchange with me, kinsman—give me this cloak and say what you will have for it."

"I do not sell what has come to me as a gift," answered Veterlide.

"Then give it me," said Ljot. "Never before have I asked anything of you."

Veterlide at first made no answer. Then Gudrun came up; she had heard something of their talk. Now she said:

"It would ill become you, Veterlide, to refuse your kinsman what he asks for—we must honour our guests. See how well we wish you, Ljot, and put off your heaviness; go out and make sport with the other lads and let us have proof of your manhood."

She bade Ljot stand up and hung the cloak about his shoulders; it suited him well, as though it had been made for him, she said. After that she left them. Ljot stood with the cloak on him. Veterlide said:

"You would not have had it but for Gudrun's words. You would be better served without it, and better still if you put her who made it out of your thoughts."

Ljot answered:

"I liked the lass well—but this time it was the cloak I liked, for it suits me finely. So I thank you for the unwilling gift, kinsman, and take what I can get."

He smiled a little as he said this; then he took off the cloak and hid it away. And now he went out into the yard, where the men were at their sports.

There were two brothers named Odd and Sigurd Beineson, and they excelled in manly exercises; Odd was the strongest man in that part of the island. Ljot was also well skilled in the use of arms and held his own, though he was somewhat out of practice. But he warmed up to the game, and at last those who were looking on said that Ljot had most skill in such sports as called for quickness and agility, but Odd was best where strength was wanted.

"I should like to see, though," said Ljot, "whether Odd is able to throw me."

The two then closed, and Ljot soon felt that his strength was far less than the other's; but then he put out all his force, and Odd trusted too much in his strength and was careless; the end was that Ljot threw him to the ground. That ended the sports for the day.

Ljot slept in an outhouse at night; next morning he lay in bed, not caring to get up; then he heard some women talking in another room. One of them said:

"How did you like seeing Odd Beineson thrown yesterday? He can no more boast that he is unbeaten."

Another laughed and answered:

"Little do I care whether Odd is beaten or not—but I am glad the handsome youth won."

"Do you call Ljot the handsome youth?" asked the first one; "Why, he has a face as brown and pale as a bogy."

"Yet he must be the one I mean," replied the other; "for I know of none other that has won against Odd."

Ljot got up and dressed himself, and then he went into the next room. There were several women, and Ljot noticed one whom he had not seen until then. She was dressed in a light-green, embroidered gown and was very beautiful; rather short than tall, but round and shapely, with small hands and feet, a fair, handsome face and gay blue eyes; but her greatest glory was her hair, for it was so long that she could wrap herself wholly in it, and it shone with the colour of flax. She was just combing it as he came in.

Ljot fell into talk with the maidens, but all the time his eyes were on the fair one. When she had done her hair he went across and asked her to lend him the comb. She gave it him; then he said:

"Was it you who called me the handsome youth?"

She blushed slightly, but laughed and said:

"How was I to know you were listening?—but you know, one wishes well and speaks well of those one has known from childhood."

Ljot was surprised at this and asked after a moment:

"Tell me your name, for I cannot say that I know you."

"Oh, that is no matter," said the maiden, and Ljot saw that she was vexed. Then he said:

"You were not half so beautiful last time we met—for now I can guess you must be Leikny Lytingsdatter."

"And none of you had eyes for me either, you and the other lads, when we were together at my grandfather's at Eyre," replied Leikny, and the other women laughed. But they could see she was pleased with his answer.

Now he was told she had been with Torbjørn for a time and had come home the day before. Ljot then asked for news of Eyre, and he had a long talk with Leikny, for she was a woman of sense and spoke well. In the evening he sat beside her and drank with her. He then said among other things:

"It is strange that you are yet unmarried, Leikny—but I suppose you think no man is good enough for you."

"Not so," she answered. "But no one takes hurt by being somewhat wary of such a bargain; I should not care to find myself so placed that I would wish myself out of it again."

Ljot laughed and said:

"You must be hard to please, and it is not I who would venture to come forward here."

Leikny made no answer to this, and they talked of other things. The next day Ljot went home.

27

Late in the autumn Gudrun gave birth to a son. Veterlide poured water on him and called him Atle. One morning while Gudrun still lay in bed, she and Leikny were alone in the room. Leikny sat by her mother's bed swathing the child; when she had finished she sat with him in her arms, kissing him and patting him, and said:

"This boy is so good and so pretty—I almost wish, mother, that he was mine and not yours."

Gudrun said angrily as she lay in bed:

"Bring him here and talk no more of such nonsense—'tis not too soon either for you to have one like him. You are now twenty; I don't know what you are waiting for, or why you cannot get married like other folk. You might have had Odd Beineson; then you would have been well off in every way, I'm sure."

Leikny answered:

"I have said once for all that I will take no less a man than one who has the good word of all."

"Then you might have listened to the suit of Runolv the *gode*,"[1] said her mother.

Leikny laughed and said:

"You cannot mean that seriously, mother. They say his house-carls have to lift the old body in and out of bed."

"You will be old yourself one day," said Gudrun; "and folk will soon be tired of being sent away like fools."

"Oh, I shall find a man in the end," Leikny answered. After a moment she said:

"If Viga-Ljot from Skomedal came here and sued for me, I would humour you and take him, though he has not folks' good word; then you need be angry no longer at my staying here."

Her mother answered:

"You will soon be as wayward as Lyting was wont to be—that is the last place I would choose to go to, if I were a maiden—in that deserted dale where nobody ever passes by."

"It is a good estate, though, as I have heard," Leikny replied. "And grandfather and all my kinsfolk would be well pleased—it is best to be on good terms with one's family."

"Yes, Veterlide would like it well," said her mother. "He would be glad to see his nephew make such a good marriage. But I had thought you should take a man who was richer and more powerful."

"Our wealth will not be so small, if we put both together," replied Leikny. "And I have always heard that Ljot had the makings of a chieftain." She was silent for a while; then she said: "Speak to Veterlide about this matter, mother—but do not say I asked you to do so."

28

Ljot stayed at home at Skomedal; just before midwinter
Veterlide came to visit him there. Ljot received him well, and
the two kinsmen had much pleasure in each other's company.

The farm lies in a valley, which is also called Skomedal; there
are high mountains on both sides, and a river runs through the
valley; at that time the slopes on the far side were covered with
birches, and there is good pasture and fishing. Ljot kept many
cattle; Veterlide looked closely how Ljot conducted his farm;
he found that Ljot was a good husbandman and much more
capable than was to be expected of a man of his age. He told
him this one day when they had been out together.

"All is so well kept here, kinsman, that I see but one thing
wanting on the farm—it is time you took a wife, one that
could manage your house; it is always better done where there
is a mistress. She may be good enough, the housekeeper you
have—but she begins to get old—and you could increase your
estate too, if you looked about for a good match."

Ljot thought the old woman managed well enough; she had
had charge of the house ever since Steinvor died. "And there
is time enough for me to get married."

"Is that what you say now?" replied Veterlide. Ljot was
silent. Then said Veterlide:

"I cannot think you still have Vigdis Gunnarsdatter in your
thoughts."

Ljot turned red and said quickly:

"Nor do I know any place where I could offer myself—I
will not be met with a nay."

"You talked with Leikny Lytingsdatter last summer," said
Veterlide. "How do you like her?"

"Well," said Ljot slowly. "She is fair, and she can hold her own in talk. But I had never thought of suing for her."

"She is just as wise as she is fair," said Veterlide; "and kind to her people and an able and industrious woman. I have spoken to her of you, and I do not believe you would meet with a nay there; her marriage is in Torbjørn's hands, and in her own and Gudrun's. To tell the truth, kinsman, I have thought you two would be well suited, and many would rejoice if this came about."

"I can see, kinsman, that you counsel me for the best," said Ljot; "and it is kind of you to wish to help me to this good marriage. But I have no desire to marry so soon."

Veterlide begged him to think the matter over, but did not bring it up again. He watched Ljot closely and saw that he slept badly at night and in many ways seemed like a man who is burdened with heavy thoughts.

The last day Veterlide was at Skomedal he asked Ljot again whether he had thought more of this matter of Leikny. Ljot then answered:

"I owe you much thanks for your solicitude, kinsman; you must help me in this matter, for I see clearly your advice is for the best."

Ljot then accompanied Veterlide home. Gudrun and Leikny received him kindly, and all was arranged for the marriage. The wedding was held in the spring, and Veterlide made it a fine one. Ljot and Leikny departed for Skomedal, and their married life went well.

29

One day in late summer Ljot was up the valley mowing the meadows he had there. It was the finest of weather and the sun was very warm. There were two men with him; they were mowing on one side of the river, but Ljot worked on the far side, and he had stripped to his shirt and breeches. They were so far from the houses that they could not go home for every meal; so, as the afternoon drew on, Ljot meant to cross the river and have something to eat with his men. Then he saw Leikny coming up the river bank; she was dressed with great care in the light-green gown she had used to wear at feasts; in her hand she carried a great bundle. She stopped to speak to the mowers, and gave them something from the bundle; but then she crossed by the stepping-stones to where Ljot was.

"Here is mead my mother has sent me," said she; "I thought it would do you good, you men who have to be mowing in this heat."

"You should not have had the trouble of bringing it here yourself," he protested.

"Oh, that is nothing," replied Leikny. "Not often do we have such weather—and I wished to see what sort of hay we are getting up here."

Ljot then suggested that they might cross the river to the mowers, who had food with them; but Leikny laughed and pointed to the bundle she was carrying:

"You may be sure your food has not been forgotten, since your wife has come all this way. But let us sit up here on the slope, where the air is soft and cool."

So saying she went up the bank, taking a handful of hay now and again and smelling it. Above the meadow was a birch copse, and Leikny had to go and sniff the fresh scent that came from the new leaves. At last she found a hollow among the rocks, which gave shade and was full of grass and heather; it was just big enough to take them both, and Leikny called him thither.

"Here you can lie down and sleep when you have eaten," said she.

They ate and drank, and Leikny was full of frolic and merriment the while. When they had finished Ljot lay down in the heather to go to sleep, putting his arm over his forehead to screen himself from the sun; on seeing this Leikny untied her kerchief and covered his eyes with it. After a while she asked:

"Can you not lie with your head in my lap?—then you will have more room."

Ljot did so. He looked up into Leikny's face, as she sat in the sunlight with her head bared, and he said:

"Now you look as you did when we met at Holtar."

Leikny smiled and said:

"Tell me, Ljot, do you think it a good thing that we met that day—or are you pleased you brought me here?"

"You may be sure I am," he answered.

Leikny went on again:

"How can I be sure? Sometimes I have thought there is something that weighs on your mind—for you are not as you were when you were a lad. Then you used to be so mad and wild and full of noise and laughter—but now there is scarcely a sound in you."

"It would not be well if one did not outgrow one's boyish pranks in time," said Ljot.

"They used to say in those days," she went on, "that you were good at singing and making ballads. Cannot you let me hear some of the lays you have made?"

"Oh, they were mostly lying when they said that," he answered. "My verses were never worth much."

"You might say them to me," she begged.

"I cannot remember any now," he said; "it is so long ago."

Leikny took his face in both hands and rocked his head between her knees, as she recited:

> "Little sleep have I for longing,
> When of the maiden I mind me.
> Nightly my thoughts fly far
> Over the murky waters,
> Resting their weary wings
> Where she lies warm in her chamber,
> She who little recks
> Of birds that fly in the darkness.
> —It steals my strength in the daytime.

—I have been told that you made this song."

"It was something like that," he answered. "I cannot remember now."

"Who was this maiden?" asked Leikny. "Was it one who would not have you?"

"Oh, it is just what one makes up," said Ljot. "One is so full of thoughts when one is much alone. It might be anyone."

Leikny thought for a moment; then she asked:

"Was there anyone you would rather have had than me?"

"No, there was not," he answered. Then she took hold of his head again, bent down and kissed him. He patted her cheek and throat.

"Well, now I will lie down too," said Leikny, and lifted his head from her lap.

"Yes, do so," said Ljot, making room for her. "This is a good place to lie." He spread her kerchief again over his face. Leikny lay down in the heather beside him, but she propped herself on one elbow and looked at him.

"It is odd how sleepy you are," she said. His shirt was open at the throat; she took a birch-twig and tickled him on the chest and under the chin. Ljot took hold of her hand and played with it a moment, but did not open his eyes.

"What is that scar you have there on your neck?" she asked. She bent over him and kissed it.

"You tickle me," said Ljot; "I am in such a sweat."

"You should go to sleep now," said Leikny.

"Yes, if you would only keep still," laughed Ljot. "I thought you said you would go to sleep too."

"Are you so tired?" asked Leikny.

"Yes, indeed I am tired," he answered.

After that they lay down, and Ljot slept, but Leikny sat up, looking at him.

30

It has been said that the valley is deserted; some house-carls and freedmen lived under Skomedal, and farther south was a farm called Svartaabakke. It belonged to a man named Aasbrand. He was poor and found it hard to make a living—ten children he had, and only the eldest son was old enough to be of any help. Halstein was the lad's name; he was big and strong, a good worker and kind to his father; but otherwise he was quarrelsome, hot-tempered and suspicious. So he was not liked. He had often picked quarrels with Ljot, for Halstein could not bear to see another man prosperous; but Ljot took it peaceably, counting the other as no more than a boy, and he was sorry for Aasbrand and ready to overlook it if Halstein took rather more than his due, whether in haymaking or fishing or in stranded goods.

Now the Svartaa[1] is the river that runs through Skomedal; its bed is narrow and deep in gullies and chasms; but just south of Skomedal it widens into a pool which has its outlet in a waterfall. But on the bank by the waterfall Ljot had his best fields, where corn could ripen. Not much rain falls in the valley, for it is kept off by the mountains, and now Ljot had it in his mind to build a dam in the stream, so that he could water his meadow and ploughland there. And he began this work one year before the spring flood. Halstein was angered, saying it would do them great harm at Svartaabakke. He went about talking to people of all the wrongs they suffered from Ljot; this came to Ljot's ears, but he laughed and said the boy could only talk as his wits would let him.

Then one day Halstein came while they were at work on the dam and went straight up to Ljot, bidding him stop the work; he was going to bring the matter before the Thing, and then it would be seen that Ljot had no right to act as he was doing and ruin a poor man's farm.

"Ay, to be sure you should go to the Thing, Halstein," said Ljot with a laugh. "Your father knows very well he will gain just as much as I by this work, for he can use my water, as much as he needs. But now go away with you; I have no time to stand here talking to you."

"You carry it high, Ljot Gissurson," answered Halstein; "for you're the biggest man in these parts. But you wait, then you'll see we have kinsmen who can take up the matter, and they may be just as good as you."

"Say you so?" said Ljot with a laugh. "Well, go on then, Halstein, and tell them from me, I'll be glad to meet them."

Leikny had now come up; she had been at the pool washing a woollen garment. She said:

"I dare say Aasbrand has been glad enough many a time that Ljot was the man he is and not too heedful—as last autumn, when we fetched in his sheep from the mountain."

Halstein turned red as fire and shouted:

"Do you taunt us with theft, Leikny?"

"No," replied Leikny; "I remember it was Ljot who brought in the sheep you could not find, and divided them between us in such a way that I believe you had good cause to be satisfied with the big man that time."

Then said Halstein:

" 'Tis a good thing, Leikny, that you are so well pleased with your husband—since you were so set on having him."

Leikny was about to answer, but Ljot said:

"You must not heed what this youngster says—and we have no time to listen to him any longer, so now be off with you, Halstein."

Halstein then left them, but he had not gone far when he turned and called out:

"You are well married, Ljot, and a good thing it was for you that you got this woman—though I have heard you were pining in Nidaros for the Norwegian girl who thought so little of your manhood that she took another right under your nose."

At that Ljot uttered a roar; he grasped a spear that lay on the ground and sent it after Halstein. It struck him in the eye, and the lad fell dead on the spot.

Ljot sent a man to announce the slaying at Svartaabakke, and then he went home. Leikny went with him. Later in the day she asked:

"What was that Halstein was saying about a woman in Norway?"

"Oh, that was an old story which you need not trouble your head with," said Ljot. "And do not talk about it to me, for I do not care to speak of it."

31

Aasbrand was so beside himself when he heard of Halstein's death that he quite lost his senses from grief and fear. He firmly believed that Ljot meant to ruin him utterly, with the dam and everything else; when Ljot came to Svartaabakke next day, Aasbrand had betaken himself to his kinsmen to beg their help. He went to the sons of Beine, who were distantly akin to his wife, and asked them to take up the case. Odd answered that Ljot was not a man to make amends for the slaying; more likely he was resolved on the worst; but Odd declared he would like to teach Ljot better manners, and as he was learned in the law and had many friends, he was willing to take charge of this case. Aasbrand stayed with Odd till it was time to go to the Thing.

Ljot also intended to go to the Althing, and Leikny wished to go with him, though he asked her to stay at home, since she was with child and it was a long and difficult journey. But Leikny wept and entreated him, saying she would have no peace at home till she saw how this would end with Odd; at last it was settled that she was to go too. They had their son with them; his name was Lyting and he was two years old. They therefore travelled slowly and came to the Thing some days late. They lodged with Veterlide, who had a booth there. He was at the Althing with Gudrun.

The day after Ljot had come, old Aasbrand was walking alone among the booths in the morning, when he met Gjest Oddleivsson and fell into talk with him. He told him who he was and of his case against Ljot. Then said Gjest:

"I have heard it was at first Ljot's intention to make amends for Halstein; but now he has turned headstrong and will not give in, because of Odd."

They talked of this for a while, and Gjest left him. Aasbrand wandered about alone for a time, thinking this over, and now he was afraid Odd might ruin his cause. Then the thought struck him to go to Veterlide's booth and speak to Ljot alone, and he did so.

They had just got up; Ljot and Veterlide sat eating with some men they knew who had looked in; Gudrun and Leikny were there too. Seeing them Aasbrand changed his mind and was going again; but Ljot called after him:

"What have you done with your backers, Aasbrand—or has Odd got tired of your case and thrown it up?"

Aasbrand stood mumbling and stuttering and at last he got out that he wished first to ask Ljot privately if he would pay for the slaying of Halstein. With that he began to weep.

Ljot then answered:

"Although Halstein has provoked me all the time we have been neighbours and no one can be surprised that he roused me to anger in the end, I yet repented of his killing, for I know he was your best help, and you are old and poor. Therefore I had a mind to offer you full weregild.[1] And if you will accept this offer at once, I stand by it. But if you take counsel with Odd I do not think you will gain much, for I will not give way to him. If you will be reconciled, I shall help you with men and what you may need at home, and neither you nor your children shall suffer any harm. Now do what you will, but remember, you are the first man to whom I have offered amends."

Aasbrand accepted the offer on the spot, and Veterlide weighed out the silver for Ljot. At parting Veterlide gave Aasbrand a silver belt, and the old man went home well pleased. But Odd was furious when he heard of it, and sent Aasbrand away with many angry words.

There was much talk of this case and folk thought Viga-Ljot had grown strangely mild of late. But Leikny praised Ljot's magnanimity to all who would listen to her—he had never been reconciled to any except to this poor old man, who had not the power to stand up against him. But they laughed at her and said Ljot could do right or wrong as he pleased, and still his wife would think it well done.

32

After the Althing Ljot and Leikny journeyed to Holtar and stayed there for a while. One day Ljot had ridden over the moor to look at a stud that Veterlide kept in that part, when he met Odd Beineson, attended by one man. Odd greeted him and said:

"As we are going the same way we might well keep company—now that you have made your peace with Aasbrand there should be no bar to our friendship."

Ljot answered merely that they might well ride together, since the other found it pleasant. Odd then asked after the folk at Holtar and how Leikny was faring. Ljot answered that they were all well.

They found the horses and looked them over; afterwards they rode back towards the valley. Odd had much to say and was friendly; Ljot gave him short answers. At last they dismounted and sat down to eat the food they had with them. As they sat thus Odd said:

"I cannot think what could have come between you and Halstein, Ljot, seeing that you are so kindly and peaceable a man—is it true, as they tell me, that it was that old matter of a marriage that you do not care to hear spoken of?"

"Since you seem to be so set on my friendship," Ljot answered, "it were just as well you did not pry into that. Or maybe you are the one who spreads the talk about it here in Iceland."

"I heard this talk from those who met you in Nidaros, while you were there pining for a maid—it was old Aasbrand, poor man, who got her marriage portion."

Ljot leapt up and seized his axe; Odd also sprang to his feet and thrust his shield before him, defending himself with his spear.

"Ay, there was nothing left for your kinsmen," said Ljot, as he cut the spear-shaft in two. "But I can find a little for you, since you are so hungry for it." With that he cleft the other's shield, and the axe sank deep into the shoulder, so that Odd fell backwards and had his death-wound.

The servant who was with Odd was young and frightened, so he ran off at once. Ljot rode back to Holtar and related what had happened. Veterlide asked what he would do now. Nothing, said Ljot; but he did not think they would have much joy of it, those who would take up the suit of Odd.

After a while Veterlide left the hall. Ljot was left alone with Leikny; only the two little boys, Atle and Lyting, were playing by the bench. Ljot flung himself down on their bed; Leikny was tidying up the things they had lying about the hall. As she did so she questioned him about the killing, but the answers he gave her were curt ones. Then she said:

"I do think you might tell me what words were exchanged between you that led to this."

"Oh, it was no great matter," said Ljot. "The truth is, Odd has had a grudge against me ever since you and I came together."

"I'm sure it was not me you were speaking of," said Leikny shortly.

"No," said he, "but it was you he was thinking of."

Leikny came over and sat on the edge of the bed; she looked at Ljot as she said:

"I do not believe you were, Ljot."

Ljot gave a little start. He was about to answer her, but she laid her hand on his breast and went on:

"This much I know, that it is not for my sake you have been so silent and doleful since you came from Norway, and it is not of me you are thinking night and day. But I know nothing of your sorrow, nor of what there is between you and Odd or between you and anyone."

He answered:

"I would rather you were content with your marriage, Leikny; and indeed I have always tried to please you. But if I had a sorrow that I hid from all, it would surely fall worst upon myself, and so you might leave me in peace."

As she was about to answer she caught sight of the cloak that Vigdis had made for Veterlide; it lay at the foot of the bed. She plucked it up and flung it across the floor, crying:

"You think ten times more of that maid in Norway who is said to have thrown you over than of me, who have never done other than the best I could."

Ljot sprang up and tried to get the cloak; but she was too quick and seized it; she ran to the hearth to throw it on the fire. He was after her, trying to snatch it, but she held it fast with both hands. Then he put an arm around her and took hold of her wrists, squeezing them till she screamed; but he did not get the cloak away from her till he had struck her over the hands with his clenched fist. Then she threw herself down and wept, but Ljot had the cloak and went out with it.

Leikny went out and sat on the threshold; she hid her face in her hands and did not see that her mother was standing by. Gudrun asked what ailed her. Leikny answered, it was nothing; but Atle clambered on to the threshold and said:

"She is crying, mother, because she was beaten by her husband—he gave her such ugly blows there by the hearth."

"That's not true," said Leikny quickly. But Gudrun went into the house and found Lyting crying on the floor, because his father had been so harsh with his mother. Gudrun was furious and rated Ljot soundly:

"That is a thing my first husband had to learn, that he must not lay hands on me," she said; "for when he did I left the house, and he lost his life when he refused to give back my property. The others have had the sense not to do the like, both Lyting, while he lived, and Veterlide."

"Be quiet, mother," said Leikny. "Ljot did not strike me—

he only dragged me across the floor, and it was I who began the quarrel."

Ljot came out at that moment. He did not listen to all that Gudrun said, but bent down and spoke to Leikny:

"I have acted badly towards you, my Leikny—and what you said is true—you have never done me aught but the best you could."

Leikny burst into tears again; she threw her kerchief over her face, sprang up and went into the house. Ljot followed her. It was not long before they came out again; but then Leikny was no longer weeping; she leaned against Ljot and looked happy.

Next day they went homeward. It had been intended that they should stay longer, and Gudrun wished her daughter to stay out the summer, till her child was born—Gudrun thought for many reasons it would be well if Ljot were away from his wife for a time. But now they were both of one mind, that they would go home to Skomedal. Veterlide and Gudrun offered to bring up Lyting with their own son, Atle, who was older by a little over a year. Ljot and Leikny accepted this; and then they left.

All went very well between them on the journey. But then came the last day; they were riding through a gap in the hills. Their men were on in front; Ljot walked, leading Leikny's horse through the pass; his own followed behind. The weather was grey and bitter; now and again a snow-squall came straight in their faces. As they made their way down in this fashion she said to him:

"I have been thinking all this time of all you said at Holtar.—But if it were so that what most grieves you is your being turned away by those folks, then it must surely console you that we ourselves sought this bargain with you—it was reckoned a good match that you made, and one for which there were many suitors."

"It is not true that I am grieving," he answered. "But you

can understand, it angers me that the sons of Beine and their friends should have this tale to carry."

"I do not understand," she went on after a while. "Why is it that you set such store by that cloak, if you are no longer thinking of her who made it?"

"Oh, it fits me so well," he answered.

The snow was now driving in their faces, so they said nothing for a while. When it had abated a little, Leikny asked again:

"Was she more beautiful than I, that girl in Norway?"

"No," he replied, looking straight out at the snow. "Most men would call you more beautiful."

"Then was she richer than I?" asked Leikny again.

"Oh, it was about the same, I think," replied Ljot as before.

"Well, but still you liked her best," said Leikny dolefully. "In what way was she better than I?"

"Oh, if there was anything, maybe she was far less fond of asking questions," said Ljot with a little laugh.

Leikny bent forward to look at him—his face was as grey as the rocks around. It was a long time before either spoke again.

The snow had ceased falling when they had come through the gap. They now had a long, flat plain with peat-bogs before them. Ljot gave the reins back to Leikny and was just mounting his horse, when she said in a low voice:

"Now this matter shall never more be mentioned between us, I promise you that; but one thing I beg of you, that you tell me her name."

Ljot stood leaning against his horse, and for a long time he said nothing, but looked away from his wife. Then at last he uttered the name, very low: "Vigdis."

After that he mounted and they rode side by side for a long time, saying nothing. But Leikny was silent and sorrowful, when they came home. It was no better with her till late in the autumn, when she gave birth to a son. Ljot poured water upon the boy and called him Gissur. After that Leikny was a little more like herself again.

33

The next autumn, when they fetched home the sheep at Skomedal, some wethers were missing. Ljot went out himself with one of his house-carls to search for them.

On the third day after this, as Leikny was standing in the yard, the house-carl came in, driving the sheep. Leikny asked what had become of Ljot. The man answered that he had stayed at the sæter to repair the walls of the hut.

Leikny went out at once and looked across the moor. The weather was fine and clear and the sun was shining on the fresh snow that covered the hillside.—After a while she told the people of the house that she thought it best to go up to the sæter—since Ljot had undertaken to repair the hut there were many things she would like to have done, and she could best tell him about them herself.

They smiled a little among themselves as she said this, but Leikny went on talking, and the end of it was that she thought she had to go. But they need not trouble to attend on her; she owned an old thrall, who had been with her since she was a child and who followed her like a dog; she took him with her, and so they set out.

They came to the hut before sunset, but saw nothing of Ljot. They could see, though, that he had cut peat in the bog that day; his spade and pick stood against the wall of the hut. They went in, and there were still embers on the hearth.

The sæter was built of stones and covered on the outside with turf, as is the custom in that country; inside there was a bench round the walls, also of stones and turf. The cross bench was broad enough for two people to lie side by side on it; a bed had been made there and on account of the smoke and the draught from the door a beam had been set up, over which skins and rugs were hung.

Leikny waited awhile, but Ljot did not come. She then told the thrall that he could go and lie down in the cowhouse. And as it was cold and there seemed to be so little fuel that she would not put any on the fire until her husband came, she went to bed and drew the curtain of rugs to keep out the cold. She fell asleep at once.

In the course of the night she was waked by the sound of a voice in the room. Looking out between the rugs she saw there was a fire on the hearth. Ljot sat on the long bench nearest her, but there was another man in the room; when he spoke she heard it was her stepfather. She listened to what he was saying:

"It seems to me an unwise thing, kinsman, to stay by yourself up here on the heath, when you have this case on your hands with Sigurd Beineson and his kinsmen. It would be a great grief for Leikny if she were to lose you, and your sons are still so young."

Ljot sat with his head leaning against the wall; he answered:

"I don't reckon them so highly as to go well attended for their sake. And I know that my death will not come from them. I know one who wished me the worst of deaths—but I believe we shall meet before that. And then I care little what else may happen."

"What is this you talk of?" asked Veterlide. But Ljot made him no answer. After a while he spoke again:

"Maybe it were better for Leikny if she were left a widow while still young enough to console herself."

"Then you know little of her spirit," replied Veterlide. "I do not believe she would take any husband after you, so highly does she honour those she loves."

Ljot sat in silence as before. Veterlide went on:

"You know well that you would not find such a wife as yours if you searched over all the world."

"That is true," answered Ljot. "But I love the black spot

she had between her breasts more than all Leikny's beauty. I
loved her more when she struck at my throat with her knife
than I love Leikny when she puts her arms about my neck. I
was less sorrowful as I rode over Dovre in wintry weather
thinking of her curses than when I ride to Skomedal knowing
that Leikny will meet me with kind words at our door. I would
rather be hugged in the clutch of the white bear than think of
Kaare holding her in his embrace."

To this Veterlide answered in great wrath:

"You have acted ill, kinsman—and worst of all when you
did not speak of this before you were betrothed."

"Yes," said Ljot; "but then I thought I could put her out
of my mind if I were once married. But now I see that, badly
as I treated her, it was even worse for myself. For now I must
grieve, as long as I live, that I possessed the fair maid and
lost her."

"I fear now," said Veterlide, "that you made an ill return
for Gunnar's hospitality."

"Worse than you think," said Ljot. "The best hour I have
known was when Vigdis and I ate berries together by the high
place—I was happier then than on the day when as a boy I
killed my father's slayer under Hauketind. But when she went
from our last meeting there, the greatest sorrow had come upon
her—though I have learnt since that I brought a greater sorrow
on myself."

Veterlide said angrily:

"If you ravished Gunnar's daughter you have done a dastard's deed that I would never have believed of you."

Ljot gave a little laugh and answered:

"Maybe I would not have believed it of myself."

Veterlide spoke again:

"This is an ill thing, kinsman—" and Ljot laughed again and
said:

"Ay, 'tis not well."

After that they were silent a long time. —At last Ljot got
up and began to undress; he asked if Veterlide did not think it

was time to go to rest. Leikny shrank close against the wall; she was shaking like an aspen-leaf, but closed her eyes and tried to look as though she slept.

When Ljot was undressed he pulled the curtain aside and was about to lie down, when he caught sight of her. He turned red as fire and dropped the curtain. Then he bent forward and called to her softly. Leikny did not answer, but breathed heavily, as though fast asleep. Ljot turned round and said:

"I must make a bed for you on the long bench, kinsman, for I see Leikny has come up."

Veterlide uttered a cry, but Ljot hushed him: "It looks as if she has slept all the evening." He made a bed for Veterlide and said nothing. Then, as he was about to lie down beside Leikny, he laid his hand on her breast to find out if she slept; he then felt how her heart thumped and fluttered like a fish in the net.

He lay down not knowing what he could say to her—so he said nothing; and that night they both feigned to be asleep, but each knew that the other was awake.

Towards morning he did fall asleep for a moment. Then Leikny gave herself up to quiet weeping, and at last she too cried herself to sleep. When she awoke the men were already up and preparing breakfast. She dressed herself quickly and greeted them. Veterlide asked when she had come and whether she had heard them during the evening. At that Ljot got up hurriedly, saying he must go and see to the horses.

Leikny answered that she had come about supper-time, had lain down to wait for her husband, and then she had fallen asleep and slept till now;—"but where were you last night, Ljot, and where has Veterlide come from?"

Ljot said he had been out seeing to his snares and had met Veterlide east in the Gagle fen; he was on his way to Skomedal and his men had ridden on ahead. Ljot took down a brace of ptarmigan from the door and asked Leikny to cook them for their meal. She did so and told Ljot why she had come. He promised to put up the shelves she wanted and to follow her advice about the hut. Afterwards she and Veterlide went down into the valley to join the men who had come.

Late in the evening Ljot came riding into the yard. Leikny stood at the door; but on seeing him she went quickly into the weaving house. He came after her and put his hands on her shoulders, making her look at him; the tears were running down her face. Then he kissed her and said:

"I know very well how happy I might be, could I rejoice in the love you bear me—there is no one so good as you."

Leikny answered:

"It hurt me not so much as you think to hear your talk last night—I had heard the worst when you told me her name on the moor here."

"How is it to be between us after this?" he asked. Leikny answered:

"It must be as you wish—with me you will always find life as you will have it."

Ljot stood for a moment with his face averted. Then he kissed her again and went out.

34

It is usually the way that time overcomes all sorrows, and so it was here—as the years went by these two had so much else to think of that even this sorrow was somewhat healed. In other ways they were always good friends; for the most part they stayed at home at Skomedal, and folk saw little of them.

Ljot and Leikny had three children: Lyting was the eldest; he was brought up at Holtar with his grandmother, and there he died while still a child. Gissur and Steinvor were the names of the others, and Steinvor was the one Ljot loved best of his children. These two met their death in an accident. It came about in this way:

One evening in spring the children of Skomedal were out playing; there were some boys belonging to the serving folk on the farm, and Gissur was with them, shooting with his bow at a mark. He was then in his seventh year, and Steinvor was four. She was playing by herself at the brook which runs past the farmyard fence down to the Svartaa. This brook is small enough to run dry in summer, but now in spring-time there was more water, and the boys had built dams in it, like those they had seen in the river. So there was a pool, which in the deepest part might come up to a short man's knees.

As Steinvor was playing about there talking to herself, she saw the evening sun shining on a bare bank on the other side of the brook. She was too small to remember the summer clearly, but she thought there must be flowers on that bank; so she waded across the brook a little higher up, where it was shallowest.

She was now quite happy on the sunny bank; she collected

stones and heather and was going to build herself a farm with many sheep and cows and horses.

After a time the big boys went in; Gissur was left alone and looked about for his sister. He waded across to her to see what she was busied with.

"Oh, it's these horses I've got to fetch home," she said, showing him a pile of yellow stones. "Can't you help me with this horse, he's so wild, I can't do anything with him." And she flung the biggest stone away and ran after it.

Gissur was quite ready to join in the game. But he thought it was a wretched farm she had made herself.

"Now I'll go over to Norway," he said, "and buy timber to build a house." He found one of her shoes, filled it with dry osier twigs and sailed it on the pool. Then they built themselves a splendid farm; but by the time it was finished the sun had gone long ago and the children were both wet and cold; so they made up their minds to go home and get something to eat. But then Steinvor had lost her shoe, and she cried at having to go through the cold water.

"I'll carry you across, sister," said the boy. He picked her up and waded into the brook.

"Look, there's father coming from the heath," cried Steinvor, and they both looked up and were going to wave to him. But there was slippery ice under the water, and Gissur lost his footing and fell with her.

Ljot came riding down by the cattleway on the other side of the river; he saw the children and waved to them. Then he saw that they fell and did not get up again; he leapt from his horse and ran straight down over the scree; in crossing the Svartaa the current nearly took him, but he reached the bank and made for the brook. The children lay quite still in the pool. He lifted them up; then he saw that Gissur had struck his forehead against a rock, and he had held his sister so tightly in his arms that she lay under him, and they were both drowned.

Ljot knew at once that they were dead; but in spite of that

he ran to the house with them in his arms and called for warm skins and hot milk.

Leikny turned white as death when she saw the children; but she said it could not be so bad, they would soon come to life again. For all they could do for them, the little ones remained dead; at last Ljot sat down by the hearth with his chin in his hands; but Leikny would not give up, she went on trying to force milk into their mouths and rubbing them with woollen cloths, though all the others told her it was now of no avail.

Then at last she gathered up the two little dead bodies in her arms and cried aloud:

"I shall bring life into them—I shall lie brooding on them till they come to life again."

She flung herself over them on the bed and breathed into their mouths. Ljot went up and put his arms round her:

"Leave them in peace," he said; "you must not treat corpses thus."

She broke away from him and shrieked again and again; she plucked the kerchief from her head and tore at her hair—then she made a dash for the door and was going to throw herself into the river. But Ljot lifted her up and carried her to their bed; he had to use force to get the clothes off her and make her lie down; all that night he sat holding her; he almost thought she would lose her reason.

But towards morning she grew calmer; when she got up later in the day she was quite quiet and did not weep much more; but she looked like one who has risen from a deathbed.

35

Time now passed sadly at Skomedal, till the Althing drew nigh. Ljot had business there and wished to take Leikny with him; but she said she was not fit to go, so he had to travel alone.

When he came home again Leikny told him she had slept in the weaving house for some nights, and asked that he would allow her to sleep there alone for a time. Ljot answered that he would not deny her that, if she wished it so much.

The summer drew to an end, and Leikny still passed her days and nights in the weaving house; she no longer busied herself with the housekeeping, but stayed there alone, walking to and fro and doing nothing. Every evening she went out to the chapel that Ljot had had built near the homestead, and there she knelt in prayer till far into the night.

But one evening, just as she was going out, Ljot came into the weaving house and asked her to stay a moment: "When did you think of coming back to me, Leikny?"

Leikny made no answer, and he went on:

"I do not think it will be any better for either of us if we are to live apart like this bearing our sorrow—you ought rather to come in and live with the rest of us and take charge of your house—perhaps that would make it easier for you."

"I have not the strength to take charge of the household," she said. "I should always think there was something I had forgotten—and when I reflected what it might be, I felt it was my children, who no longer need me."

Ljot answered:

"Then do you wish to go home and visit your mother?— if so, I will take you there."

Leikny said quietly:

"One thing I wish above all—if you would let me have my greatest wish."

"Nothing will I deny you, whatever you may ask," he said.

"It is that I may never more be your wife," said Leikny. "Grant me that I may go from here and live in chastity and fasting, as women do—elsewhere in Christian lands."

Ljot frowned and said:

"I know you have not been too happy here with me—and never would I have brought you hither to Skomedal had I known how it was to be. But once I asked you how it was to be between us, and you chose to stay with me. And since then I have tried to do as well by you as I could, and there has never been an angry word between us from that day, and never have I laid a hand on you since that one time. In all things here you have had the say as much as I, and I have never meddled with your doings. I have not sported with other women and I have not had children by any other than you."

"You have no children by me either," replied Leikny. And now she hid her face in her hands and wept.

"That is as great a sorrow to me as to you," he said; "and I wonder therefore that you now wish to break off our life together."

Leikny rose to her feet and answered:

"You must declare our marriage at an end—it must be ground enough that I refuse to live with you. You can then marry another wife and leave this wilderness—never a day have I seen you happy in all the years we have lived together here."

Then Ljot asked in a low voice:

"Tell me truly, Leikny, if it is so that you long to leave this place, and would you rather I never shared your bed any more?"

He drew her down on to his knees as he said this, and now she was trembling so that she could not answer. He said again:

"You once said that with you I should always find life as I would have it."

Leikny laid her face against his hand and answered in tears:

"I thought you wished to go from me."

Ljot lowered his face to hers and said:

"That is long ago, Leikny—but I did not know then that I cannot live without you."

The same evening Leikny went with him into the hall and sat at her table as before. There was no more talk of her wishing to become a nun; but she and Ljot lived together in great affection and unity. But she still grieved much for her children, though she did not speak of it.

One evening they had all been to the bath-house, and Leikny let her hair hang loose to dry it. Ljot gathered it in his hands and said:

"I believe your hair is fairer now and more beautiful than it used to be, Leikny."

She turned red as fire and quickly drew her head away. But Ljot saw that there was now as much grey as yellow in it and that it was quite white at the temples.

36

A year went by; then Ljot found that Leikny often lay awake weeping at night. He asked her kindly what ailed her; but she would not tell him. Once he said:

"I do not think you will be really happy again till the child you go with be born." But at that she wept still more.

One day he came into the storehouse; Leikny was on her knees there, tidying the contents of a great chest. Ljot begged her to spare herself, saying he did not see there was need of this.

"Yes," she answered; "I will leave my house in order; I must do it while I can."

"Do not speak so," said Ljot, with a forced laugh; "do you think maybe you are going to die?"

He made her sit beside him on the chest. Then she answered:

"Every day they walk about the floor, Gissur and Steinvor, and try to get up into our bed, and the water runs off them. And they will have me come down and lie beside them and take them in my arms. I tell them I cannot because of this child. But they answer me, when this our brother is born you must come to us and warm us, mother, for you have promised us that."

"This is something you have dreamt," said Ljot. "You know very well that our children are with God; it is only heathens who walk the night like that, but they were baptized and lie in Christian ground. Do not talk like this and put it out of your thoughts," he begged her again.

"I see them as clearly as I see you now," she replied. "They have come up and taken hold of me; they were so cold that it froze my marrow."

"Oh, that is the wind," said Ljot, taking her in his arms; "I will have the wall mended behind the bed. But you must not talk of dying now—the children are well, where they are, and I have more need of you than they."

Soon after this Leikny gave birth to a boy. Ljot kept asking the midwives how it was going; but they answered, all was as well as it could be. But when the child was born and they carried him in to his father, he was such a wretched babe that they told Ljot he ought to have him exposed, "for there will never be a man of him, only a miserable cripple, so he will have no joy of his life."

"That were an unseemly deed, since I am a Christian man," replied Ljot, "and I will never do it. God may help the boy and mend him." He had the child baptized and called him Torbjørn.

Leikny wept when she heard this; she too thought it would be better if the boy did not grow up. He had a hare-lip and no roof to his mouth; and his right hand was small and withered and strange to look at. She said so, but Ljot laughed and answered he did not think the left hand was so big either.

It went well with Leikny and on the tenth day she got up, but that evening she had fever and had to take to her bed again. Next day she was not so well. Ljot sat with her that evening. Then she said to him:

"I am afraid it will fall out after all as I have feared the whole time—though I have prayed that we two might not be parted now. I am grieved for two things—that you should have this poor sick son, and that this did not happen at the time when you would not have mourned my death."

Ljot kissed her and answered:

"I do not believe in your dreams and visions—and the greatest joy that has been mine is the good time we have lived together—whatever may happen."

Leikny fell asleep, and Ljot sat by her all night. Towards morning she suddenly started up in her bed and pointed with both hands to the door. Then she threw her arms about his neck and fell backwards, dragging him with her. The next moment she loosed her hold and lay stretched out in the bed; she was dead.

Ljot mourned his wife deeply; but folk thought he bore his loss in manly fashion and made little complaint. He took care of the boy himself and loved him greatly. He always said he believed the boy would grow out of his infirmities, but the others thought among themselves it would be better if he died. Torbjørn lived through the winter, but convulsions took him before spring was out.

At the Althing that year Ljot gave out that he wished to sell his estate; he bought a ship and left the island. In Normandy he parted from the Icelanders he had had with him from home. After that no more was heard of him in Iceland.

37

After King Olav Trygvesson had fallen, Illuge the fair came to Oslo; he would serve no other chief after that flower of all the men who have lived here in the Northern lands. Illuge now desired to settle and take a wife. He sued again for Vigdis. Vigdis received him well and made a great feast; she also asked Kaare of Grefsin to come to it. To both these men she showed the greatest honour.

One day she bade them go with her into the storehouse, for she wished to speak with them alone. She then said:

"You have both sought me in marriage—and it is a far greater honour than I could expect, that two such gallant and noble men will have me to wife. But I will not marry—all I desire is that my son may have wealth and be so placed that he shall not feel too deeply the lack of father and kin—and he shall not have to share my estate with true-born children. And both of you have been so good to me that I cannot prefer one before the other. Therefore this is my advice: you, Kaare, shall give your sister Helga to be wife to Illuge, and Illuge shall buy Baugstadir[1] beyond the ridge; but Kaare shall make his suit to Ragna Grjotgardsdatter, my kinswoman, whom you saw here today. These are the handsomest and richest maidens here, and if you enter into bonds of friendship, you two as brothers-in-law can rule together over the whole country-side. Now I beg you to listen to this advice and tell me what you think."

Kaare spoke first:

"Gladly will I have Illuge for brother-in-law, if he will do as you say; I believe it would be for the good of both of us if we concluded this bargain. I shall not show myself a niggard when I give my sister in marriage."

115

Illuge answered:

"Then you shall bind yourself to Ragna the same day as I drink my betrothal with Helga."

Kaare made no answer, but Vigdis said:

"Trust me, I shall never marry—but now you two could both add to your wealth and power if you made this bargain. You may well count yourselves equals, so one will hardly,outstrip the other—but if you hold together your strength will be doubled."

Kaare then held out his hand to Illuge, who took it, and they agreed further upon the matter.

Vigdis turned aside and opened a great chest full of precious things; she bade them take from it what they would have.

"Grant me now to enjoy the friendship of you both—and I have this boon to ask of you, that you will train Ulvar in the use of arms and in manly conduct, so that he may grow up like one of you."

They promised this and thanked her for her rich gifts. All who had been present at this feast were given costly things on their departure, and Vigdis won great respect thereby.

38

At the church which Vigdis had built there was a priest named Eirik. He was from Denmark. Vigdis liked him well, and he often came to Vadin.

One evening when he was there and they sat round the hearth after supper, Vigdis asked the priest to tell them a story, for he knew many.

The priest then began:

"There was once a woman in Odinsø.[1] Her name was Tora and she was very fair. So it befell that she was seduced, and seeking to hide her misfortune she cast the child into the sea.

Afterwards she made a good marriage, lived respected and beloved and had many children, of whom she was very fond. But then she fell into a grievous sickness and swooned away, so that she lay as one dead. While she lay thus it seemed to her that she was dead, and she was clothed and adorned and laid in the burial mound;[2] but she could hear her little children weeping for her at home in her house, and she fervently desired she could find means of going home to comfort them. Then it seemed to her that one came into the mound; he was wrapped from head to foot in a black cloak, and he took her by the hand, saying: 'Rise up, Tora, and come with me.' Now she no longer felt that she was dead, and she begged that she might go home, where her children were crying for her. The man in the cloak nodded and led her with him. 'But this is not the way we are to go,' said Tora. 'Yes, this is the way,' replied the man.

When they had gone a long way they came to a deep, dark valley; there was a black river at the bottom of the valley and a sheer cliff down to the water, and on the other side there

was also a sheer cliff. But on the mountain there stood a castle
of pure gold; it shone like the sun, and outside it stood knights
in golden armour, and within the castle they sang and played
upon harps, so that she had never thought that anything could
be so beautiful. She asked who was the master of the golden
castle. 'I am the master there,' said the man. 'Will you come
with me, Tora, and see my house?' Yes, she would come
gladly, but afterwards she would go home to her children.

They began to go down the mountain-side. Then it looked
to her as if the valley were full of little white lambs; they stood
as close as in a fold, they crawled and climbed, trying to get
up both sides of the ravine. But when she came nearer she saw
they were little children; there were many thousands of them;
they were quite naked and newly born, but their faces were
old, and some were bloody and horribly mangled, and some
were wet. They tried to climb out of the valley on both sides,
but they rolled back again at once, for they were so small and
weak. This seemed to Tora such a sorry sight that she began
to weep; she asked him in the cloak what it was and how the
poor little things had come there. 'Their parents have left them
here,' said the man. 'They willed it so.' 'I can never believe
it,' said Tora.

The children had the power of speech, and they said: 'It is
true, and now we must lie here. Gladly would we come up
and see the world, and gladly would we see the other world
on the far side of the valley; but we are so small that we must
stay here, and it is so bare and ugly, and we are so cold.'

Then Tora took off her cloak and tore it in pieces; she
wrapped the nearest ones in it. Now they all crowded about
her, so she took off her outer garment and shared it among the
children, and so she went on till she was left as naked as they.
And yet there were just as many who had received nothing;
there were many thousands of children in the valley. All this
time they went forward, and the children swarmed about her,
begging her to carry them up, that they might see how the

world looked. 'Oh, there is indeed no delight in seeing it,' she said. 'Yet they are so loath to be rid of life, those who come hither,' said the children. 'They all wish to go back again— and so do you.' 'I only wish to go home to my children,' said Tora.

Now they came to the water, the man and Tora. And it too was full of little children; they stood with the water up to their necks, as thick as a shoal of herrings, and they shivered with cold and caught hold of Tora. She felt so sorry for them that it made her weep, and she gathered them up in her arms, as many as she could carry, and she asked the man if she might not take them with her to the golden castle. She might indeed, the man answered. Soon she could carry no more. Then she asked the man to lend her a cloak that she might wrap them in it. He took it off, and then she saw that under it he wore a splendid armour of gold with a cross of precious stones on his breast and a gleaming crown on his head. But his face shone even brighter, and it seemed to Tora she had never thought any man could be so handsome and kingly.

Then he said: 'Here the slope is so steep that you cannot come up it unless I carry you. Shall I carry the children first, or you?'

'Take the children first,' she said. 'If you cannot carry them all together, I can sit here and wait meanwhile.'

'That will be a long time,' said the knight; 'you see how many there are here—and more are coming all the time. You wished to see my golden castle, and after that you wished to go home to your children. But here you may sit till the end of the world, before I have brought all these children home to me.'

'Then I must wait, however long it may be,' said she; 'I have not the heart to leave these poor little children here; mine are well at home, so these have greater need of our help.'

Then said he in the golden armour:

'It is your eldest son, Tora, who is now lying next against

your breast—all these are children who have been robbed of life before they could live in the world or learn the way to my house.'

Tora fell on her knees and asked in terror:

'Who are you, chieftain, and what is your name?'

'Christ is my name,' said the King. And now a radiance went out from him, as though the sun had risen upon the valley, warming all the children. But Tora had to shut her eyes before the glory of it. And when she opened them she was at home, lying in her bed.

She sent at once for her husband and her kinsfolk and told them of her vision, and she no longer concealed the disgrace that had lain upon her, nor that she had made away with the child. Her husband was so furious that he bade her get up and quit the house at once, though it was the middle of the night.

Now she fled through the town, and all the dogs barked at her; she thought she was so unhappy and had sinned so grievously that she ought not to live. Therefore she went down to the shore. Then she heard a sobbing between two great boulders; she followed the sound and found among the sea-tang a new-born man-child; it was still alive. Tora wrapped it in her clothes, put it to her breast and let it suck. She then resolved she would foster this child. She went far away among the woods till she came to a part where they did not know her. She built herself a hut and lived there with the child. Afterwards she secured all the silver and gold that were hers, and gave out that she would foster all the babes that would have been exposed. She sold all she possessed and bought food for her foster-children, but she herself for Christ's sake ate only the grass that grows upon the earth and drank water from the brook. When monks came to the country and preached the faith they were greatly surprised to find her, knowing the Lord's name and honouring him in her life. She was then baptized, she and the children; and when she died she was called a holy woman on account of her penance."

Vigdis thanked the priest for this story; when it was over she sat in thought the rest of the evening. At bedtime, as her people went out, she called to Ulvar. He was now nine and very fond of his mother; he sat on her lap and put his arms round her.

"Would you have sat waiting for me in that valley till the end of the world, mother?" he asked. "I almost think you would."

Vigdis squeezed him in her arms and said:

"I too learned that one night, as did Tora. I too would go to the world's end to save you, when you really needed your mother."

The boy kissed and caressed her. After a while he said:

"You never would tell me who was my father."

"You are not to remind me of him when I am happy," his mother answered. "And you are not to ask me about him."

"When I am grown up," said the boy, "I shall go and seek him out; and then he shall be forced to marry you, or he will regret it."

Vigdis answered with a little smile:

"It is a good while before you will be grown up, my son, and a long time before I let you go. We will never speak of him, and never shall he set eyes on you and do you harm; but you shall have the best I can give you, and I will forget what I cannot bear to remember."

Ulvar grew apace and became a handsome and promising lad. He was tall of stature, but rather slight of body and limb, with a narrow face, light blue eyes and long, sooty-brown hair with a tinge of red in it. He early acquired a manly bearing, for while he was still a boy his mother discussed with him all that concerned the work of the farm and their welfare, and asked his advice; she treated him as though he were fully grown and had knowledge enough to support her. This made him some-what serious and sparing of words, but he was gentle and cour-teous in his manner and well liked. He and his mother lived together in the greatest affection.

But when he asked who was his father, she would never answer him. She said she had nothing good to say of that man, and she hoped never to hear his name again. Afterwards she was always heavy-hearted, so Ulvar dared not question her further.

Kaare and Illuge and Vigdis remained good friends, and every year each of the three made a feast for the others. They looked after Ulvar and trained him in all manly sports—he was more often at Grefsin, as it was nearer; but he was never more happy than when he could ride to Baugstadir, for Illuge had seen much and Ulvar liked to hear all he had to tell.

One evening when he was there Eirik the priest came to Baugstadir, and Illuge asked the priest to tell them something to pass the time. Eirik then told the story of the holy Gregorius, who slew the dragon in Kampedus. Illuge said:

"Next after Christ, who overcame the Devil, this is the greatest feat of prowess—only two can compare with it— Sigurd Sigmundsson, who slew the serpent Fafni,[1] and Olav Trygvesson, who did not flee from three armies at Svold.[2]

There has not been his like since the grey old days of legend, and men can scarcely look to see such a chieftain while the sea breaks about these Northern lands."

Eirik answered that Olav was indeed the greatest chieftain in that part of the world—but now he would tell them of the courage of holy martyrs and of sufferings bravely borne for the faith in Southern lands—and to show them the valour of the faithful he would tell of a young maid's steadfastness. He then told them the story of the holy Agatha.[3]

Illuge said:

"A great heart had that maiden, and never will her fame be forgotten. But now I will tell you of the most gallant woman I know of—you, Ulvar, must have heard something of this story, but I'll warrant you never heard the whole."

He then told of Vigdis' journey through the forests on the night Vadin was burnt. He did not utter her name, but when he had finished he said to the boy:

"Do you know of whom I speak—or do you know of any woman who lacks the three fingers of her left hand?"

Ulvar nodded and took the other's hand. Illuge said:

"If you take after your mother we shall hear great things of you one day."

When Ulvar rode into the yard at home next day, Vigdis was there, feeding the foals with bread. Ulvar leapt from his horse, ran up and threw his arms around her. She laughed and asked what had come to him.

"Nothing," he answered; "only that I believe, mother mine, that you have no equal—" and with that he raised her left hand and kissed the stumps.

"What has Illuge been telling you now?" asked his mother, laughing again.

"Do you know what I have in my mind?" Ulvar went on. "It would have been a good match if you had taken Olav Trygvesson; you two would have suited each other well."

Vigdis turned red and said nothing. She kissed her son on the cheek, and then she bade him go in and eat.

40

One evening two Icelanders, traders on their way to Tunsberg, came to Vadin and asked for a night's lodging. Vigdis received them well and entertained them bountifully. They were men of good breeding and gentle manners. Vigdis sat talking with them till late in the evening.

She asked them at last whether they knew anything of a man called Viga-Ljot, and whether he were still living.

Yes, they answered, they had heard of Viga-Ljot of Raudasand, but he was killed before they were grown up.

Vigdis said it could not be so long ago, "for I can remember when he was here in Norway."

Then one of the chapmen said to the other:

"Did not folk call Ljot Gissurson of Skomedal thus—at the time he avenged his father, while he was yet but a boy and was herding sheep for Eyre-Torbjørn?"

Vigdis said:

"He was called Ljot Gissurson, the man I speak of. Do you know if he is alive?"

Ulvar was sitting on the bench; he leaned over the table and begged them:

"Tell us of that—of him who avenged his father while he was a boy and herded sheep!"

Vigdis glanced at her son and said nothing. One of the men said:

"You must tell it, Helge, if the lady of the house wishes to hear it."

"We do indeed," said Vigdis in a low voice, dropping her eyes. "You must tell us the story, if you are not tired."

Helge began:

"This Ljot was the only son of Gissur, who was killed by Gunnar the wealthy of Gjeitaabakke and his kinsmen; there were eight men with Gunnar, and one of them was Arne Kollsson;[1] it was he more than any who brought about the slaying. Gunnar paid weregild, and indeed folk thought they had conducted the suit well, those who appeared for Gissur, for they were of small account at that time compared with Gunnar and his kindred. But no one was able to take up the case against Arne. Ljot was then about two or three years old.

Then came a day in winter, when Ljot was thirteen; he was up in the fells with some other boys searching for a sheep that they had not brought down. The boys sat under a ledge of rock eating, and they all boasted of the feats they could perform. Ljot claimed he was now so good at throwing the short spear that he never missed his mark. Then one of the lads pointed into the distance and said: 'Do you see that band riding up the valley under Hauketind?[2]—I make out that it's Arne Kollsson crossing the heath. If you could hit that mark, Ljot, it would be a better price for your father's death than Gunnar's gold.'

The boys had three short spears with them. Ljot took them all and ran northward over the mossy flats. The mountain road through the valley becomes a narrow track; at its narrowest it runs along a ledge with a sheer wall on one side, three or four times the height of a man; on the other side is a steep scree of rocks. Ljot made for this and hid behind a big rock a little way up the scree. Arne now came out on the ledge; there were four men riding with him. The path runs steeply uphill. When the men were right under where he lay, Ljot jumped up on to the rock and flung the first spear. It struck the man who rode next to Arne. Ljot leapt back behind the rock again; the men had not seen who threw the spear. They stopped and looked about them. Ljot leapt up on the rock again and shot the other two spears; one of them missed, but the other killed a man who stood in front of Arne. Ljot cried out: 'Now I am better off than my father, Arne, for you were eight against him, but now you are only three against me.' He had a little woodcutter's axe in his belt, and as Arne scrambled up behind the rock, Ljot struck him on the crown from above, and the axe lodged in the man's lower jaw. Then there was one who flung a long spear at the boy, but he caught it in the air. And now he ran up the scree, keeping behind the rocks so that they could not take aim at him. When he came to the edge he planted the spear and swung himself over the gap—then he ran along the brink of the cliff till he was out of the pass. There he found the riderless horses. Ljot seized one by the bridle, leapt on its back and rode home to Eyre, where he was then living.

But everyone thought this the greatest feat that had been performed by a boy, and many foretold that he would become a famous fighter, and so they called him in jest Viga-Ljot."

Vigdis asked after a while:

"Do you know, Helge, what has become of him since?"

"Oh," said Helge, "little has been heard of him these last years—since he married he is said to have grown more peaceable."

"Is he married now?" asked Vigdis in a low voice.

"Yes," replied Helge.

"Do you know his wife?" she asked again.

"I have seen her, no more," said Helge. "She was counted the fairest maid in those parts and a rich and kind woman—so since he got her to wife he has kept quiet at home on his farm."

Vigdis was silent for a while. "Do you know if he has children too?" she then asked.

"Yes, they have three or four, I have heard," replied Helge.

Vigdis then said no more.

But when the Icelanders had gone to bed, Vigdis stood by the hearth, staring into the embers. Ulvar was sitting on the bench. Then she said, without looking at him:

"Did you listen to all these men had to say?—now you have had news of your father."

Ulvar sprang to his feet and cried:

"Was he my father?—he who killed the three men in the mountain pass when he was no older than I am now!"

"That was your father, he who has the handsome wife," replied Vigdis.

Ulvar said:

"Whatever he has done to you, mother—he must be a manly fellow, and glad would I be to meet him one day—then he should find that he has a son who takes after him."

She answered:

"If you take after him—and if you are son of mine, then the end of that meeting must be that you brought me Viga-Ljot's head and laid it in my lap."

Ulvar turned pale—and then he said:

"Never yet was such a thing heard of as a son slaying his father."

Vigdis raised her hands and clasped them upon her breast; she answered:

"Will you not avenge me, as I avenged my father?—and you must know that I have suffered so unspeakably through him and he has treated me in such a way that if I told you all you would have no peace till you had wiped out the score— or your love for me is less than I have thought. But I cannot bear to speak of it any more."

Ulvar came over and embraced his mother, and now she laid her head on the bench and wept. Then the boy made answer that she might be sure he would always do as she willed in everything.

41

Time went on, till Ulvar was seventeen years old. Then he spoke to his mother, saying he had a great desire to travel abroad and see the world. Vigdis thought this reasonable, and promised to fit him out a fine large ship; but she wished him to sail in company with older, experienced men.

When Illuge heard this, he declared that he might be glad to go to sea again, now that his wife was dead, and there was much talk of the matter.

One day towards the end of winter Illuge came to Vadin; he sat alone in the hall talking with Vigdis, and she asked him what were their plans.

Illuge said:

"You know, I doubt not, that the first course Ulvar would follow is to Iceland."

Vigdis made no answer, and Illuge went on:

"I dare say you can guess what would take him to that country—but you can hardly be surprised that I have little wish to make this voyage with him."

Vigdis said in a hushed voice:

"Ulvar has been much with you and has talked with you of many things—has he spoken to you of his father?"

"Many a time," replied Illuge. "His mind seems set upon meeting him, to see what sort of a man he is. What do you think of it; have you advised him to this?"

"No," she said. After a moment she spoke again: "Ljot does not know that I have a child. I would rather he gave up this voyage."

Ulvar was passing the door at that moment; Illuge called to him, and said, when he came in:

"We are speaking of your Iceland voyage, your mother and I."

Ulvar turned red and said hurriedly:

"You can hardly be surprised, mother, that I desire to meet the man who begot me, and to see how he receives me."

"He has never sought news of us," she said angrily; "and he has wife and children in his own country; you will hardly reap anything but scorn if you seek him out."

"Then I cannot be your son," Ulvar answered in wrath; "if I let myself be scorned—before now you egged me on to vengeance; you said once it would make amends for all, were I to lay Viga-Ljot's head in your lap."

With that he went out. Vigdis said hotly:

"Rather would I never hear his name again."

Illuge looked at her and answered:

"Great must have been your love for this Ljot, since you still hate him so fiercely—I almost think you love him yet."

"I love him as dearly as I love the wolves of the forest," said Vigdis. "Were we to meet, it must be the death of one of us."

Illuge answered:

"Is it so that you would gladly be avenged on Ljot?"

"It is so," she said.

Illuge then said:

"I shall go with Ulvar to Iceland, and I shall watch over him as though he were my son. But then I shall ask you to marry me when we come back."

Vigdis did not answer at once. Illuge then went on:

"Do you not think you have stayed long enough as a widow, sorrowing over the falseness of this man—you are still young and handsome and may yet have many happy days. You know well that I will be good to you and will help your son with all my power."

Vigdis then gave him her hand, and he kissed her; and all things were settled for their marriage. She told Ulvar of this, and he said his mother must decide for herself.

42

As it fell out Ulvar did not reach Iceland. In the North Sea they met with fogs and head winds, and after that a gale sprang up, so violent that they had to throw most of their goods overboard if they would save their lives. At last they lost their rudder, and in the heavy weather they could not keep the ship on a course, but drifted to leeward towards a rocky coast, which Illuge said must be Scotland. They then set some sail and steered with the oar; thus they slipped in among the islets, where there was less wind and the sea was slighter, and in the evening they cast anchor in a bay, where there was a sandy bluff at the mouth of a river and high hills around. There were no houses that they could see.

During the night the wind increased in force, so that the ship dragged her anchor and ran aground, but the men got ashore safely. Illuge said that if those who had the shore rights came, they would certainly be killed; his advice was therefore that they should see to making the ship seaworthy and sail away.

They worked at this the whole day, and towards evening they were ready for sea. But as they were short of food, Ulvar was for making a raid inland. Beyond the bay was an inhabited valley, which they followed; they stopped at the first large farm, drove the people out and took what they wanted of food and clothing. There was no one to oppose them.

But when they came back to the shore they saw that their ship was full of men, and Illuge said they must be the Scots who had come round by another way and had overpowered the men they had left to guard the ship. And at that moment they caught sight of a great band of horsemen riding down through the valley, the way they themselves had come. Illuge said:

"How do you like this jaunt, Ulvar?"

"At least it is better sport than getting soaked through by the seas," replied Ulvar with a laugh. "But now we'll have to scramble on board and throw the men out of the ship, before this greater force overtakes us."

Illuge said it would be far easier first to drive off the Scots who were coming down the valley than to get on board the ship, "for they will hack at our hands as we climb up the side—but we need not trouble much if these horsemen outnumber us."

"I'm not afraid of them," said Ulvar; "but it would be worse if they took our ship and sailed away; then we should be left here like a fox in a trap."

And now he and most of his men leapt into the water, holding their shields over them to ward off the arrows from the ship, as they waded out to her. But Ulvar was soon to learn that it was not so easy to get aboard, for the Scots could hack and shoot at them from above. Although the Norsemen advanced bravely and sent back the spears as fast as they were flung at them, they gained little ground, and now the Scottish horsemen were riding out into the water; thus they had the enemy on every side, and they themselves were up to their waists in water and were hard pressed. Ulvar now said to Illuge:

"Your advice was best, foster-father."

"You're as good as two, Ulvar," said Illuge; "and it were a pity Vigdis should lose such a son." With that he dashed in under the ship's side; standing on the bulwark was a tall redhaired man who was leader of the Scots. Illuge threw away his shield, made a leap and got up, catching the Scottish leader by the legs; but as he did so the other struck him on the head. They both fell into the water, and Ulvar killed the Scot. This confused his men at first, and some gave way from the bulwarks, but others sprang overboard after their chief. And so many of the Norsemen succeeded in getting aboard the ship.

Ulvar was the last, for he wanted to help Illuge up. But
Illuge said:

" 'Tis no use—but see you save yourself, for I would have
you bring a greeting to your mother, that she may hear how I
met my end."

"She would be little pleased if I came home without you,"
replied Ulvar; he reached the bulwark, and now they were able
to pull up Illuge after them; but he fell forward on the deck
and was dead. Now Ulvar was on board his ship; he still had
thirteen men, but not one unwounded, and the Scots were
more than half a hundred; they pressed about the ship, and
while some hacked at the ship's sides, letting the water in, their
comrades held shields over them and sent one flight of arrows
after another at the Norsemen.

Then Ulvar caught sight of a great ship bearing straight
down on them within the islands. Ulvar called to his men:

"Short was this voyage of ours—but we may be well pleased
at our evening's work," for the Scots had lost heavily.

Now the strange ship cast anchor, and her men jumped
overboard and made for Ulvar's. Foremost among them was a
tall, dark man; he struck a grappling-iron into the bulwark and
swung himself up. He ran forward to the mast, where Ulvar
stood, calling out in Norse:

"Well fought, young chieftain! Lucky are we that can help
such brave fellows!"

In a moment the ship was full of his men, and now the tide
of battle turned against the Scots; they leapt into the sea and
made for the shore, but not many of them reached land.

The fight being over, the stranger threw the fallen Scots
overboard and had Ulvar's ship towed out alongside his own.
It was then seen that she was so badly damaged that she could
not float. The stranger therefore invited him and his men to
come aboard his ship; they set sail and stood out to sea. They
now had a good breeze, as the gale had abated.

The stranger bandaged the wounds of Ulvar and his men
and heard the whole story of the fight. He said his name was

Uspak¹ and he was born in Iceland, but he lived in Northumberland, and his crew were Norsemen and Danes from that
country.

When darkness fell they cast anchor in a sound and went to
rest. Uspak and Ulvar shared the same couch below the deck.
Ulvar lay awake, for his wound gave him some pain, so Uspak
talked to him. He said:

"You fought like a man today, Ulvar, and you surely come
of a good stock; where in Norway is your home, and whom
do you call father?"

Ulvar answered:

"My home is in Vingulmark;² Vadin on Folden is the name
of the house I come from."

Uspak turned to him abruptly and asked:

"And your father, Ulvar—what is your father's name?"

"I will not hide it from you, chief, that I was born out of
wedlock," said Ulvar. "Therefore they call me Ulvar Vigdisson
after my mother."

Uspak was silent a long time; more than once he was about
to speak, but could not get out the words. But Ulvar did not
notice it. At last the other said:

"How old are you, Ulvar Vigdisson?"

"I shall be eighteen after midsummer," he answered.

The stranger lay down again and said nothing for a long
time. Then he spoke again:

"Is she still alive, your mother, and is she still unmarried,
Vigdis of Vadin?"

Ulvar answered that it was so. Uspak said:

"Gladly would I hear more of your mother—she must be a
woman of great mettle to have brought you up alone to be the
man you are. Is she fond of you, your mother?"

Ulvar said:

"When I was fifteen years old she gave me Vadin and half
of her goods to be my own, so that no one might cast poverty
and weakness in my teeth, although I am a bastard. She cleared
a farm for herself to the north in the forest. Berg is the name

of it; but she lives at Vadin. And you are right, she is the most
mettlesome of women; I do not think there is any like her, and
I believe I have lost little by not knowing my father."

Ulvar then told the story of his mother, and the more he
told, the more the other questioned him; thus he heard all
about Gunnar's death and Vigdis' revenge and what had happened since; and much of the night was spent in the telling.
When he had finished Uspak said:

"You owe your mother a vast debt of kindness; she ought
to receive the greatest affection and honour from you. It seems
to me she is unmatched for courage and wisdom, and no
woman has loved her son more."

"That is true," answered Ulvar. "I hope some day I may
reward her for her goodness."

Uspak said:

"You have now lost your ship and your goods; but if you
will stay with me this summer, you need not return to Norway
a poor man in the autumn; you shall share the command of
this ship with me and half the chief's lot shall be yours."

Ulvar thanked him heartily. After a while he said it had been
his purpose at first to sail to Iceland. Uspak asked if he had
business there. Ulvar said:

"As you come from Iceland, Uspak, do you know a man
they call Viga-Ljot Gissurson of Skomedal?"

"Have you a message for him?" asked Uspak after a pause.

"I might have," said Ulvar.

"Perhaps he is a friend of your mother?" asked the elder
man.

"A friend he is not," replied Ulvar; "and little good do we
look for from him. But I should like to see what sort of a
welcome he would give me, for I am told he is my father."

"He must be a strange man," said Uspak with a little laugh,
"if he be not glad to greet so fine and manly a son, and scarcely
can he have forgotten a woman like your mother."

"Never has he sought news of us," replied Ulvar; "and I
know that he has wife and children in Iceland; but I should

like to bring him a greeting from my mother, whom he seduced and left in the lurch."

Uspak said after a pause:

"He is no longer in Iceland, Ljot; I have been told he left that country many years ago—his wife and children died."

"Was he a friend of yours?" asked Ulvar.

"No," said Uspak. "He was no better a friend to me than to your mother."

Ulvar now settled himself and tried to sleep. After a while he felt that the other touched him and passed his hand over his face. Ulvar opened his eyes; the other had then opened the hatch, so that the morning light shone in on him, and Uspak sat bending over him.

"You stirred in your sleep, Ulvar," he said; "I wanted to feel how it was with you; but lie down now and sleep."

43

Ulvar was with Uspak till late in the autumn; together with Danish vikings they harried the coasts of England, Kinnmare-land[1] and France and carried off much goods. Ulvar Vigdisson showed great courage and won renown thereby.

In the autumn Uspak and Ulvar were with Earl Sigvard in Northumberland; he was Uspak's friend, and he received Ulvar well and gave him great gifts.

One evening the two sat together in Uspak's lodging drinking. Then Uspak asked:

"Is it so, Ulvar, that you would gladly find your father?"

"While I lived at home," replied Ulvar, "that was my greatest wish; it grieved me that I was a bastard, and I thought I must be of less worth than all those who had a father to be proud of. Then I always thought I would seek him out and crave amends for my mother and myself and all the wrong she has suffered."

"It might happen that you found him," said Uspak in a low voice. "What if he received you with affection, rejoicing that he had such a son?"

"He could hardly count that to his honour," Ulvar answered; "and I should not thank him for it; I do not know that I owe him more than my bare life—and that I have already ventured too many times to count it of much worth. Here abroad I have learnt that I am good enough without him—and that I owe chiefly to you, Uspak. I do not need my father, and I do not ask for his love—and it is no matter to me whether he be a dastard or what he may be."

Uspak sat listening with his head in his hand; after a pause he asked:

"And your mother—what if he were to hear of you and came and sought Vigdis in marriage?"

"To speak the truth," replied Ulvar, "I believe he might spare himself that trouble. She said once that it would heal her suffering if she could hold in her hands his bloody head. But at most times she has been loath to speak of him, and it always made her low-spirited long after. It was not to her liking that I set out for Iceland to find him."

Uspak sat as before. At last he said:

"That was a hard saying, Ulvar."

Ulvar answered:

"And it was a hard lot he assigned to my young mother, when he sailed away and left her behind to bear his child. And never has he sought news of her since."

"Are you so sure that he has not sought news of her since?" said Uspak.

"She has told me often enough," replied Ulvar, "that he was the worst and most heartless of men."

"Those are hard words from a son, Ulvar," said Uspak again, with a sigh.

"He has taught me none better," replied Ulvar with a laugh; "and maybe I take after him too."

Uspak looked at him, but made no answer, and no more was said of this; but Uspak was silent and thoughtful that evening. Before they went to bed he took out of his chest a red silken cloak, handsomely embroidered with gold and silk, and handed it to Ulvar; he bade him accept this gift. Ulvar thanked him.

When Ulvar was ready to go home in autumn, Uspak gave him a fully found ship and rich gifts besides—a long coat of mail and a golden helmet, two snow-white falcons, a trebly gilt girdle, which he asked Ulvar to give to his mother in token of friendship, and finally a green silken cloak with a gold clasp and lined with costly fur—but then he said he wished to have the red cloak back, as it was not new and he no longer thought it suitable for a gift.

Ulvar thanked the other for all the affection he had shown him and asked Uspak to choose what he would have of all the booty he had taken on his summer voyage.

"I have more goods than I need," replied Uspak. "But I would gladly have that ring you wear on your left arm as a remembrance of you, if you will grant me that."

Ulvar took off the ring and gave it to Uspak, saying:

"It is of no great worth—I wear it as it was given me by my mother, who had it from her mother—but it is too poor a gift; ask me for something better."

"I will have nothing else," answered the other, stroking his hand with it; "for I like it, and you wore it on your arm when you defended yourself so well in the Scottish fjord."

Ulvar then said:

"At Vadin we do not keep a house like that of the Earl, but it would give us the greatest joy if you would visit me in my mother's home."

"I will surely do so," answered Uspak; "and it shall not be long before we meet again, for I would have come if you had not asked me."

After that he took Ulvar in his arms, kissed him on the lips and forehead and bade him fare well. Then Ulvar sailed home to Norway and landed in Folden on the fourth day.

44

Vigdis received her son with great joy and was never tired of hearing of his doings. Above all Ulvar told her of Uspak, who seemed to him the greatest of men and the best of friends; then said Vigdis that it would be her greatest joy to receive him, though she thought she could never fully thank the man who had saved her son's life and shown him such great kindness.

She was deeply grieved over Illuge's death and made a feast in his memory; she then promised to bring up his children, Olav and Ingebjørg, as though she had been their mother. They lived after that at Vadin.

Now the year wore to an end and the feast of Yule[1] came round. And in the holy night, when Our Lord vouchsafed to be born, folk came from all the country round to the chapel to hear Mass; and from Vadin Vigdis and Ulvar rode with a great company.—That year much snow had fallen before Yule, and it was cold weather with a full moon during the holy days.

So strong was the moonlight that it seemed dark in the church, as Vigdis stepped over the threshold with her son, although the candles were burning before the holy images. The priest sang sweetly before the altar, and the choir-boys swung the censers, spreading fragrance. Those who entered bowed the knee and crossed themselves with holy water, as they said their prayer.

But when Vigdis lifted up her face and rose to her feet, she saw there was a man standing by the wall near the door. He was wrapped in a dark cloak, which he held together under his chin, and his head leaned slightly forward, so that she saw no more of his face than the eyes under the dark hair which came down over his forehead. But she knew him at once for Ljot.

He stared at her, and when he met her eyes she saw that his hands began to tremble so that he let them drop; and then he was as pale as a dead man.

Vigdis herself was shaking so that she had to lean against the doorpost, and it seemed to her that the floor began to sway before her eyes—it was no longer a floor, but a red river running between the men and the women, and before the altar there was a lake of blood. Ulvar rose to his feet at that moment, and he bowed to the stranger and gave him his hand, smiling with joy—and now Vigdis guessed who this man must be that called himself Uspak. Then she tried to go forward, but she had not the strength to walk up the aisle; she made her way along the wall, steadying herself with her hand on the timbers, till she reached the corner, and there she was about to kneel; but the women made room for her, so that she might come up to the altar. She turned her face round and saw that Ljot was still standing by the door with his eyes fixed on her, and Ulvar was at his side. Then she went on and fell on her knees by the altar-rail, resting her head against the wall and hiding her face in her hands.

As the singing rose and fell around her, Vigdis was thrilled through with waves as of ice and fire, and she trembled with terror at this meeting. It now seemed like yesterday, that evening when they first saw each other and all that had happened between them. All that had grown up with the years slipped away from her, as a landslide scrapes the trees and growth from the mountain-side till the rock is left bare, and it seemed to her that all these years she had only been waiting for the game to be played out between them.

The longer she knelt there the more terrified she was of speaking to Ljot. There was an opening low down in the wall where she was kneeling and the wooden plug had been taken out; she saw the snow shining outside and heard the horses neighing and jingling their bridles in the close; and then, in the middle of the Mass, she got up and fled from the church.

Outside the moon stood high in the heavens; Vigdis ran

across the snow to where the horses were tethered and took
hers out. She led it to the churchyard fence, when two men
came after her in such haste that they left the church-door open
behind them, and the lights and the singing flowed out after
them.

Ljot seized her horse by the bridle, just as she was riding
away; he said:

"Grant me to speak with you, Vigdis—"

She looked down on him and answered:

"Are your misdeeds now so many, Ljot, that you are forced
to hide your name?"

Before Ljot had time to answer she jerked her horse away
so sharply that he had to let go, and now she made off to the
northward as fast as the horse could gallop. When she came to
Vadin she did not stop, but turned her horse and rode on, till
she came to Berg. No one lived there but a bailiff with his
wife and a few thralls. Vigdis went into the hall; it was almost
empty, for the houses were quite new; there was nothing else
but the bare bench round the walls and a table. She had a fire
made on the hearth and ordered the door to be barred. Thus
she sat there alone that Yule night.

45

When Vigdis had ridden from them, Ljot and Ulvar stood for a while watching her go. Then Ljot threw his arms around Ulvar, kissed him and said:

"May God bless you, my beloved son, for now I do not know if we shall meet again."

Ulvar took his hand and kissed it, saying:

"I do not know what you mean—but if it is true that you are my father, you will not leave us now?"

Ljot answered:

"It is so that I may not look to have speech with your mother, and the words you once uttered of your father were not too hard. That evening I would have told you who I was; but then the thought came to me that I would speak once more with Vigdis, before I called you son of mine. But this I must tell you, that I did not know of you until I heard you call her your mother—and now tell Vigdis that she is well enough avenged in that I am to lose you, and that I have never been happy since she and I last met."

Then Ulvar embraced him, begging and beseeching that he would go with him to Vadin; Vigdis would not forget that Ljot had saved his life and given him such loving help. At last he agreed, and they rode to Vadin; but Vigdis was not there. Ljot then sank forward on his horse's neck and said:

"You see now, Ulvar, it is no use—I may well call myself Uspak, for no man has acted with less prudence than I—and now it is too late for me to amend what I have done."

Ulvar leapt from his horse and begged Ljot to go in:

"Mother must be at Berg; but come in now and take some food and rest."

For Ljot looked miserable. Ulvar brought him in and seated him in the high-seat; but Ljot scarcely touched the food and did not utter a word. Therefore Ulvar said, when the day was somewhat advanced, that he would ride to Berg and speak with his mother, while Ljot stayed behind at Vadin.

But Ljot stood up and said:

"This matter must now have its end, as it is fated, for nothing else will come to pass. And now I will speak with her, as I have longed to do these seventeen years."

With that he went out and mounted his horse, and they rode to Berg as fast as they could.

There they found the door barred, but Ulvar went up and knocked at it, crying:

"Open, mother, I have weighty matters to speak of."

"Are you alone?" asked Vigdis from within, after a moment.

"My father is with me," answered Ulvar.

"I will not speak to him," said his mother again.

Then Ulvar cried:

"I demand to know, mother, from you and from him, why I am fatherless—I will not go from here, and Ljot shall not leave this place, until you open."

Vigdis then unbarred the door and let them in. Ulvar looked from one to the other; he said:

"Grey-haired is my father now, and you, mother, have grown old under the eyes—much have you two gone through since you last met; if what has been done amiss could now be mended, then were I well served, for I bear great love to you both."

Vigdis raised her face and said:

"My eyes have grown old with weeping, and none has caused me more sorrow than you, Ljot."

He answered:

"Yet has yours been the better lot, Vigdis, living here with your son—and I understand you could not love me, after the way I failed you; but you did not feel my absence. But I have sorrowed at every step I took, every wave I rode over, since it did not bring me nearer to you."

Vigdis gave a hard laugh and said:

"What of your wife—how does she like this jaunting abroad to visit your women?"

"She was the best of all and most worthy of love," said Ljot. "Now she is dead, and a sad time she had while we lived together; it was you who were always in my thoughts and little affection did I show her. More heavily than all the rest she weighs on my mind, for all joy was taken from her without fault of hers—but you can take comfort in that you were fully avenged, since I have seen my fair children die by mischance before my eyes and have lost all my dear ones, as you prayed I might."

At this Vigdis grasped her cloak in both hands, so hard that the clasp broke in pieces on her breast, and she cried:

"How should you know, Ljot, how great was my wrath—or you, my son, how painfully I have yearned for vengeance? —for I have never heard of a man being ravished by a woman. Nor can you tell what it is to be powerless, feeling within oneself the growing child of the man whom I would fain have seen torn asunder by wild horses. It was not you who tried to find the river in the dark winter night, when I knew no other way out of my misery. Do you think he owes you great affection, this boy whom I bore one night on a bed of stone in the forest—while there was not *one* at hand to give me a drop of water in my sharpest pain? —You sailed and you rowed and you longed for me; that was a great help to me when they brought in Gunnar to me bleeding, with his death wound and with scorn on his lips for the shame that had been put on him against my will. And much did your love help us, your boy and me, the night they burnt Vadin and my father, and I fled with him on skis through the great forest, and the wolves drove us to a den of outlaws.

"Perhaps you think you made full amends when you came later and were so kind as to offer to take me with you to Iceland—and when I did not accept with thanks you took another maid, who was rich and handsome enough for you, and plagued the life out of her—while I sat here unable to answer my father when he taunted me, or my child when he asked about his father; for I could never bring myself to speak of what you had done to me. Ill do you reward those who have loved you—and truly, Ljot, you are the most stupid of men and the worst."

Ljot's face was white as the driven snow as he answered:

"Your tongue cuts sharper than did your knife when we last talked together; and gladly would I now lose my life, if that would comfort you—but still I tell you, Vigdis, that my sorrow was as heavy as yours—for you do not know how miserable is the life of one who longs for his beloved."

"It is true," she said, "I know no more of love than you taught me that evening by the high place, and since then I have been afraid of every man who has wooed me."

Ulvar now put in a word:

"It was ill luck that you two ever met—but bear in mind, mother, that he saved my life, and no father has shown his son greater affection than he has shown me." With that he burst into tears.

Vigdis looked at her son and said:

"Do you remember that you once promised to avenge me?"

Then Ljot spoke:

"I had thought that we might be reconciled for Ulvar's sake—but I see you cannot forgive me; I have wronged you too deeply for that. Now I shall go back to the place from which I came; but Ulvar is to have all I possess."

Vigdis cried:

"You once took everything from me, and now you come back and rob me again. I exposed it to the wolves and eagles, the child you forced me to bear—our thralls found it and kept it alive. Afterwards I came to pity him, for he was as helpless as I was against you. I saved the boy, and was maimed myself in doing it, and I have brought him up and loved him for eighteen years—now you come and will take him from me."

"I will not take him from you," said Ljot. "He shall follow

you and obey you, for I have no right to him—but surely you
will not grudge him to be loved by me too, or that I may do
him what good I can—I shall see him no more."

"Nothing will I share with you," she said, raising her
maimed hand; "and I will not have a child of yours. Now
choose, Ulvar, to which of us you will belong."

"I cannot choose," Ulvar answered in tears.

"Then you have chosen Ljot," said his mother, going to the
door. Ulvar ran up and put his arm round her:

"Where are you going, mother mine?"

She answered:

"I do not know. It would have been better that we two had
not escaped with our lives that night in the forest, than that I
should be left crippled and old and live to see you go from me
with a stranger. In truth you take after your father, and it is no
wonder you choose him."

"Mother," cried her son, "you well know I will do all you
wish of me, and never will I see him again."

"I do not know whether I am your mother," she answered;
"the boy I bore in hatred and wrath would never have shown
your nature—you are more like Æsa and the race of thralls;
you give way at once before one who is stronger than
yourself."

Then Ljot came up to them, and his voice trembled as he
said:

"I do not know whether he is my son, or Kaare's of
Grefsin—but do as your mother wishes, Ulvar."

Vigdis turned to Ljot—but he seized Ulvar by the arm and
went out hurriedly with him.

46

Ljot and Ulvar rode down through the forest, and they did not look at each other, nor did they speak. But at last Ulvar said:

"I had never thought you would part from my mother with an insult—seeing how shamefully you have treated her in the past."

"Oh, it is as she would have it," replied Ljot. "It is but fair that she should have her way for once."

With that he leapt from his horse and tethered it; he took his sword and shield and bade Ulvar do the same. Ljot said the high place was near by; they could go there, where they would be undisturbed. Ulvar made no answer, but followed him, and they walked a short way through the snow.

When they came to the high place Ljot chose a ground which seemed suitable for fighting. Ljot made the first stroke, and it fell upon Ulvar's shield. Then Ulvar said:

"I have seen you strike better than that, Ljot."

"I am weary and fasting," he answered; "but you are young and untried in single combat, so we may call it even. Strike hard, for I do not mean to spare you—Vigdis shall have the fight she has provoked."

Then Ulvar struck at him, and as he did so Ljot threw down his shield and grasped his sword with both hands; Ulvar's stroke fell upon his left shoulder, making him drop his arm and stagger backward against a tree, leaning his head against the trunk. Ulvar threw down his sword and shield as he saw the blood gushing from Ljot's wound, and his face was pale as he said:

"That is enough—I will fight with you no more."

"Oh, enough it is not," answered Ljot, sinking to his knees. Ulvar had turned so that the sun was in his eyes and he did

147

not see clearly what next happened. But Ljot took hold of his
sword and set the hilt against a stone with the point towards
his breast; he threw himself forward and rolled over on his side
in the snow.

Ulvar sprang forward, bent over Ljot and raised him so that
he sat leaning against a stone. Then said Ulvar:

"Never would I have borne arms against you, had you not
said that about Kaare of Grefsin."

Ljot smiled in death; he answered:

"I thought that, and therefore I said it. But do not grieve
over this; for it was my own doing, that it had to end thus.
And God be with you, son, that you may not inherit our for-
tunes. Now do as your mother wishes; long have I yearned
that my head might lie in her lap."

The next moment he shrank together and died.

47

Vigdis walked to and fro in the hall; she took her cloak about her and threw it off again, although the cold was so severe that the frost sparkled on the walls. Then she seated herself by the hearth, but again and again she got up and went to the door; at last she stood there looking out, as the sun sank red into the frost-fog.

Then she saw a man ride out of the forest; she knew him for Ulvar, and he was alone and rode at a foot-pace—her knees began to shake under her, and she went back and sat by the fire again.

She could not bring herself to look up, when she felt that Ulvar opened the door. He carried a bundle in his hands and laid it heavily in her lap, went past her without speaking and into the bedroom; he bolted the door from within.

Vigdis remained seated, passing her hands over what she held on her knees. It was wrapt in a red silken cloak, which she knew again; it was the same she had made long ago and given to Veterlide Glumsson. It was frozen stiff, and it crackled when she took hold of the ends to unfold it. Then she stopped and sat as before. But after a while the bundle began to thaw, so that blood and water oozed through and wet her lap. Vigdis drew aside the cloak, and now she was looking at Ljot's head, which she held in her hands.

The first she saw was the stump of the neck; then she turned it over, so that the face lay upward. The hair had fallen forward and clung fast to the skin; she pulled it away and wiped off the bloodstains with the hem of the cloak. Once she passed her hand over his lips—they seemed to her poor and shrunken, as they stood out, blue and pale, against the grey face. She raised the eyelids and looked at his eyes; but they were dead and stupid, and she closed them again.

She was reminded of the hour in which she had stood over Eyolv Arneson—then she had tasted the sweet and bloody drink that had the power to slake her sorrowful heart. But the longer she looked at Ljot's head, the sadder was her mood; for his face was so old and full of affliction; it seemed to her that this poor wretched grey head was no atonement for her misfortunes—it was not worth enough to let her say, it was for this hour she had striven and laboured for all these years, since her father died.

Vigdis covered the face again and laid the bundle on the floor by her foot. She got up and went to Ulvar's door; but there was no answer when she called to him. Then she waited awhile and called again, but it was useless; and she went back and sat down with her hands in her bloodstained lap.

Thus a great part of the night went by; then Ulvar opened his door and passed through the hall; he did not see his mother, as the fire had almost gone out. He was dressed for a journey and went out into the yard. Vigdis rose and followed him. Ulvar led his horse out of the stable and saddled him. Vigdis came forward.

The moon shone brightly, and never had his mother thought Ulvar so like Viga-Ljot as when she saw him now, as pale as the dead man. She would have questioned him of the fight, but dared not. So she said merely:

"Must you ride away?"

"Yes, I must," answered her son.

"Will you ride to Vadin?" his mother asked again.

"I shall ride farther tomorrow, for I have no desire to stay in these parts," he said.

Vigdis looked up into his face. She asked once more:

"Is it that you will not stay with me any more?"

"I have now rewarded your affection, mother, in the way you once bade me," replied Ulvar. "I do not know what further comfort you will have of me, so you may well let me go now."

"Do not speak thus," his mother begged him. After a while she spoke again: "If it is so that you would rather be spared the sight of me, I will stay here at Berg as long as you please; but do not go away now in the middle of winter."

"I cannot bear to stay here any longer," said Ulvar. "Now that my mind dwells on all the horrors of this place, I know I could never more be happy here."

Vigdis threw her arms about the horse's neck and leaned against him. She dared not ask Ulvar to stay, and her heart sank within her heavy as a stone, for she saw that this could not be averted. So she clung to the horse, and suddenly she thought of the night when she gave birth to her son, and of the horse which was the only living thing she had to lean upon.

"Do you love me no longer, son?" she asked in a low voice.

"I do love you," replied Ulvar. "But now you must let me go, mother." After a pause he said: "I beg you for my sake to see that Ljot be decently buried."

"I shall do so," answered Vigdis.

Ulvar said again:

"You are not to thank me for his death—he was his own slayer."

With the reins in his hand he asked all at once:

"Answer me one thing truly, mother mine—did you ever love him, Viga-Ljot?"

She burst into tears and laid her face against the horse's neck as she answered:

"I could not have hated him so long—it was the worst of all, that I would rather have loved him than any man."

Ulvar leaned forward in the saddle, raised her face and kissed her on the lips. Then his mother asked:

"Will you come back home to me some day?"

"If I live," answered Ulvar, "I will surely come back some day. But let me go now, mother."

Vigdis then let go the horse, and Ulvar rode away.

Vigdis Gunnarsdatter lived on at Berg after this. She caused Ljot Gissurson to be buried outside the church she had built, and she lived ten years after him. She sat alone and saw no one; but in the last year, when she was sick, Ingebjørg Illugesdatter came to her and stayed at Berg till she died. Olav and Ingebjørg had Vadin after her; she had disposed it thus, but they were to give the estate back to Ulvar, when he returned, or to those who might be his rightful heirs.

But no news of Ulvar Ljotsson ever reached the Oslo country, so it is thought that, as he had promised his mother to come back and no one has heard more of him, he must have lost his life somewhere abroad in the world. Olav and Ingebjørg thus kept the estate, and they have made gifts both to the church that was built of stone on the hill above the river Frysja, after the wooden chapel had been burnt,[1] and to the stone church that was built to the north of the Great Lake. This was dedicated to Saint Margreta,[2] and since then the valley about this lake has been called the Margretadal.[3] By that church Vigdis Gunnarsdatter lies buried.

EXPLANATORY NOTES

CHAPTER 1

1. *Gissur Hauksson of Skomedal:* Old Norse surnames are patronymics;
   that is, Gissur Hauksson means "Gissur, son of Hauk." Should
   Gissur have had a sister, her surname would have been Hauks*datter*
   (or *dottir,* in the Icelandic form). Surnames, therefore, do not get
   passed on; Gissur's son is called Ljot Gissursson, not Hauksson.
   This system can get confusing, as families usually honored their
   ancestors by reusing their names. The father of Norway's King
   Olav Trygvesson (who plays a role in this novel) was named
   Trygve Olavsson; three generations later, another man named
   Trygve Olavsson claimed a right to the Norwegian throne as the
   illegitimate son of Olav Trygvesson. Obviously, names alone could
   not make it clear which generation or even (since there were also
   other Olavs and Trygves) which persons were meant. In Gissur's
   case, "of Skomedal" (*dal* = dale or valley) helps identify the family
   by its address, in this case the valley of the river Svartaa. Icelandic
   bards always began their sagas by reciting genealogies; that way
   the cast of characters was made perfectly clear.
2. *Eyre:* Peninsula on Iceland's west coast.
3. *a-viking: Vik* = bay or inlet. Norsemen from the eighth to eleventh
   centuries became known as "Vikings" because of their practice of
   raiding by sea—harrying and plundering foreign settlements along
   coasts, bays, and rivers from their flexible, seaworthy longboats.
4. *Viga-Ljot:* Ljot the Killer (Ljot is pronounced "Yot"). Colorful
   nicknames were common in Iceland (historical figures in the sagas
   include Unn the Deep-Minded, Olav Peacock, Thrand the
   Squinter), providing another way to identify individuals when patronymics were confusing.

CHAPTER 2

1. *Romerike:* District about 25 miles northeast of Oslo.
2. *Folden:* Old Norse name for the Oslo Fjord.
3. *Frysja:* A small river, now called the Aker, which runs through and under the modern city of Oslo.
4. *Vadin:* Today Vøyen, on the west bank of the Aker (Frysja) in Oslo's center.
5. *high-seat:* The "throne" of the manor house, the largest and most elaborately carved piece of furniture a family owned. It was reserved for the patriarch or for honored guests.
6. *house-carls:* free servants, most often found in the royal court. That Gunnar has house-carls testifies to his status as an important chieftain.
7. *Ran's daughters:* Ran (= plunder) was the goddess of the sea who caught drowning sailors in her net. Her nine daughters all had wave names.
8. *bower:* From *bur,* a farm building with sleeping rooms. Norwegian farmsteads consisted of several detached buildings; unmarried women had their own separate quarters.

CHAPTER 3

1. *runes:* The twenty-four runic characters were probably derived from the Etruscan alphabet as early as A.D. 300, and were used for inscriptions and magic incantations in parts of Germanic and Anglo-Saxon Europe until 1200 (see Introduction). At the beginning of the Viking Age (800–1100) the alphabet was reduced to sixteen characters, reflecting a linguistic change in Scandinavia.
2. *priestesses at the high place in the grove:* This "high place" (*horgen*) was a pagan religious sanctuary where blood sacrifices and other rituals were performed. Such sanctuaries were sometimes made in groves, sometimes on flattened hilltops. Recent scholarship, however, disputes the idea that Norse cults ever used priestesses.
3. *Blaaland:* "Blueland," the land of "blue" or black people, referred to any country beyond the Mediterranean.

CHAPTER 4

1. *decide her marriage for herself:* Undset has done here what many of the saga writers also did: injected a Christian practice in a setting where it hardly could have been known, and certainly was not yet observed. In the pre-Christian period Norse women did not choose their own husbands. Gunnar might well have thought it prudent not to cross his daughter's wishes, but he does have the final word. The mingling of pagan and Christian marriage customs appears several times in this novel. For more about the cultural shift see Sigrid Undset, *Saga of Saints* (New York: Longmans, Green, 1934); Jenny Jochens, *Women in Old Norse Society* (Ithaca and London: Cornell University Press, 1995); Judith Jesch, *Women in the Viking Age* (Woodbridge, England: Boydell Press, 1991); and Birgit and Peter Sawyer, *Medieval Scandinavia: From Conversion to Reformation, circa 800–1500* (Minneapolis: University of Minnesota Press, 1993).

CHAPTER 5

1. *took her on his knees:* When a man placed a woman on his lap, he was following established steps in courtship rituals of the time. The gesture had serious implications, which helps explain why Vigdis is frightened to tears. See Jenny Jochens, *Women in Old Norse Society*, pp. 70–71.
2. *Norns:* The three goddesses of Fate in Norse mythology.

CHAPTER 6

1. *Grefsin:* Today Grefsen, in central Oslo, on the opposite side of the Aker River from Vøyen (Vadin).
2. *Trondheim:* City in the Trondelag district on the west coast of Norway, at the mouth of the river Nid. Trondheim was the seat of medieval Norwegian kings from the time of Olav Trygvesson's reign. In 1030 (i.e., in Vigdis Gunnarsdatter's lifetime) King Olav Haraldsson (the Saint) was buried in Trondheim; his shrine at the

Nidaros Cathedral became one of Europe's most important pilgrimage sites in the high Middle Ages.

3. *Earl Haakon of Lade:* Chief ruler of the Trondheim district ca. 970–95. A conservative heathen who vigorously resisted Christianity, Haakon was the country's last pagan ruler. His arrogance and penchant for abducting other men's wives led to a revolt of the farmers in his district. According to Snorri, after an all-night standoff in 995 Haakon's own thrall Kark "cut off the earl's head and ran away with it. Next day he entered the estate at Hlathir and presented the earl's head to King Olav" (Snorri Sturlason, *Heimskringla: History of the Kings of Norway*, trans. Lee M. Hollander [Austin: University of Texas Press, 1964], p. 192).

4. *King Olav:* This is Olav Trygvesson, Norway's great folk hero and first Christian king, who reigned 995–1000. Olav was captured by pirates as a child, sold as a slave in what is now Estonia, and discovered there and taken to Russia, where he was raised by the queen. In young manhood he made viking excursions with Danish kings in Britain, where he was baptized by a hermit fortune-teller and confirmed at Easter, 995, in London. That same year he returned to Norway, determined to convert his homeland (see Introduction).

5. *Sløngve:* Sling. The name comes from a horse belonging to the Yngling king Adils in Snorri's *Heimskringla*.

6. *Grimelundar:* West of Vadin, on the opposite side of the river from Grefsin.

7. *Aarvak:* Vigilant.

8. *if we tried our horses together:* Horse fighting *(hestekamp)* was a very ancient custom in the North. A picture stone found in Sweden suggests it dates at least from the Migration Period (ca. 300–600). A number of Norwegian place names are derived from sites used for this purpose (cf. Undset's *Hestløkken*, Chapter 10). The first written references to horse fights appear in Norwegian and Icelandic laws in the late thirteenth century. They also occur in several sagas, including *Njals Saga*, from which Undset clearly borrowed here. Ritual horse fights (which lasted into the nineteenth century in Norway) were bloody contests that conformed

EXPLANATORY NOTES   157

to strict rules; the winner earned great social prestige and the loser great shame. See Svale Solheim, "Hestekamp," in *Kulturhistorisk leksikon for nordisk middelalder* (Copenhagen: Rosenkilde & Bagger, 1956), vol. 6, pp. 358–59; also *Horse-fight and Horse-race in Norse Tradition*, Studia Norvegica no. 8 (Oslo: Aschehoug, 1956).

CHAPTER 9

1. *the men from home who are at his court:* Icelanders who counted the Norwegian kings as allies often stayed for extended periods at the royal court. Among those who could have been there when Ljot was at Vadin are several historical figures known from the sagas: Leif Eiriksson (the Lucky), who made the first expedition to North America around this same time; Kjartan and Bolli, both lovers of Gudrun Osvifsdottir in *Laxdæla Saga*; and Kolbein from *Njals Saga* (Snorri Sturlason, *Heimskringla*, pp. 215–16).

CHAPTER 10

1. *Hestløkken:* Horse paddock.

CHAPTER 11

1. *scald:* Poet.

CHAPTER 12

1. *Hakedal:* About 15 miles north of Oslo.

CHAPTER 14

1. *sæter:* Like farmers in many mountainous countries, Norwegians practice transhumance, the custom of moving livestock seasonally. The *sæter* is a small farm building (cf. Swiss *chalet*, Icelandic *shieling*) used by dairymaids when cattle are grazing at higher altitudes; milk, butter, and cheese are sent down to the main farm period-

ically. During the winter the *sæter* is left stocked with provisions so it can be used as shelter by wayfarers.

2. *freedman:* A freed thrall, or slave. Scandinavian slaves, who were often captives, were a hereditary group used both as household servants and farm laborers. Freed slaves had lower status than the fully free, and many continued as servants of their former owners or cleared forests and became tenants (Birgit and Peter Sawyer, *Medieval Scandinavia*, pp. 131–32).

CHAPTER 15

1. *Tunsberg:* An important Viking trading center on the west side of the Oslo fjord.

CHAPTER 16

1. *night-and-day: Viola tricolor,* wild pansy or Johnny-jump-up.

CHAPTER 17

1. *Sealand:* The largest of the Danish islands, directly across the sound from Skaane, in southern Sweden.
2. *Öland:* One of two large islands off the southeast coast of Sweden where Viking and medieval culture flourished.
3. *Southern Isles:* The Hebrides.

CHAPTER 19

1. *Æsa Haraldsdatter:* Up to this point in the story we have had no knowledge of Æsa's personal history. Now that her parentage is known, she is given a patronymic, Haraldsdatter.

CHAPTER 21

1. *leman:* Mistress, concubine.

CHAPTER 22

1. *Great Lake:* The source of the river Frysja, today called Mari-dalsvannet.

CHAPTER 24

1. *Bear Lake:* Near Kikut in Nordmarka, between Oslo and Hakedal.
2. *Hadeland:* Beside the Randsjford, about 40 miles north of Oslo.

CHAPTER 25

1. *Thing:* Regional assembly of chieftains where legal disputes and other civil matters were adjudicated (see Introduction).
2. *Ulvar: Ulv* = wolf.

CHAPTER 26

1. *Leikny:* Dexterity, skill.
2. *Althing:* The national assembly of the Icelandic republic. It met annually on the plains of Thingvellir, in the southwestern part of the country.

CHAPTER 27

1. *gode:* A chieftain who performed the functions of a priest in pagan Iceland.

CHAPTER 30

1. *Svartaa: Svart* = black; *aa* = river. The Svartaa empties on Iceland's north coast.

CHAPTER 31

1. *weregild:* Fine paid to settle a lawsuit (see Introduction).

CHAPTER 37

1. *Baugstadir:* Today Bogstad, near a large lake of the same name several miles northwest of Vøyen (Vadin), within modern Oslo city limits.

CHAPTER 38

1. *Odinsø:* Today Odense, a city named for the god Odin, on the Danish island of Fyn.
2. *burial mound:* Between the Early Bronze and Viking ages stone or earth mounds (*hauger*) were erected over most Norse gravesites. They varied widely in size, shape, and elaborateness. *Hauger* were often ritual centers (cf. the "high place" where Vigdis's ancestors practiced their magic). The first description of Viking burial rituals was written by Ibn Fadlan, an ambassador from Baghdad who spent more than a year among the Norsemen in 922. See Michael Crichton, *Eaters of the Dead: The Manuscript of Ibn Fadlan, Relating His Experiences with the Northmen in A.D. 922* (New York: Knopf, 1976); also James Graham-Campbell, *The Viking World* (New Haven, Conn., and New York: Ticknor & Fields, 1980).

CHAPTER 39

1. *Sigurd Sigmundsson:* Sigurd the Dragon-slayer of Germanic legend, who rescued the Niflung gold from the dragon Fafnir (a story freely adapted for Wagner's *Ring* cycle). After Sigurd's death his widow, Gudrun, married Atli (Attila the Hun) (see Introduction).
2. *Svold:* King Olav Trygvesson was killed in September 1000, in a naval battle at Svold on the Baltic Sea (probably near Rügen), where he fought three armies of Danes, Swedes, and rival Norwegians. According to legend, Olav did not die. A champion underwater swimmer, he was said to have made it safely to an island and been sheltered by a noblewoman; from there he wandered to a far-off land to live out his life as a holy man.
3. *holy Agatha:* A third-century virgin martyr from Sicily, who suf-

fered cruel tortures for refusing the sexual advances of the Roman magistrate Quinctanius.

CHAPTER 40

1. *Arne Kollsson:* Not to be confused with Koll Arnesson, enemy of the Norwegian Gunnar.
2. *Hauketind: Tind* = peak.

CHAPTER 42

1. *Uspak:* Imprudent.
2. *Vingulmark:* The area around Oslo.

CHAPTER 43

1. *Kinnmareland:* Holland.
2. *Yule:* Name derived from *jul*, the Norse winter solstice festival; after the region's conversion to Christianity, it became the name of the Christmas season.

CHAPTER 48

1. *church that was built of stone . . . after the wooden chapel had been burnt:* The stone Aker Church, dating from ca. 1080–1100, still stands atop earlier wooden building remains on a hill above the Aker (Frysja) River near Vøyen (Vadin). If Ljot Gissursson was buried there, his ghost could have watched the courtship of Undset's characters Kristin Lavransdatter and Erlend Niklausson begin in that same churchyard two centuries later.
2. *Saint Margreta:* A third-century virgin martyr from Antioch, tortured by the prefect Olybrius for refusing to break her vow of celibacy.
3. *Great Lake . . . Margretadal:* The same lake that Vigdis had fled across the night of Gunnar's death. On the outskirts of modern Oslo, it is now called Maridalsvannet, and the stone ruins of Margreta Church can be seen beside it today.

FOR THE BEST IN PAPERBACKS, LOOK FOR THE

In every corner of the world, on every subject under the sun, Penguin represents quality and variety—the very best in publishing today.

For complete information about books available from Penguin—including Penguin Classics, Penguin Compass, and Puffins—and how to order them, write to us at the appropriate address below. Please note that for copyright reasons the selection of books varies from country to country.

In the United States: Please write to *Penguin Group (USA), P.O. Box 12289 Dept. B, Newark, New Jersey 07101-5289* or call 1-800-788-6262.

In the United Kingdom: Please write to *Dept. EP, Penguin Books Ltd, Bath Road, Harmondsworth, West Drayton, Middlesex UB7 0DA.*

In Canada: Please write to *Penguin Books Canada Ltd, 90 Eglinton Avenue East, Suite 700, Toronto, Ontario M4P 2Y3*

In Australia: Please write to *Penguin Books Australia Ltd, P.O. Box 257, Ringwood, Victoria 3134*

In New Zealand: Please write to *Penguin Books (NZ) Ltd, Private Bag 102902, North Shore Mail Centre, Auckland 10.*

In India: Please write to *Penguin Books India Pvt Ltd, 11 Panchsheel Shopping Centre, Panchsheel Park, New Delhi 110 017*

In the Netherlands: Please write to *Penguin Books Netherlands bv, Postbus 3507, NL-1001 AH Amsterdam.*

In Germany: Please write to *Penguin Books Deutschland GmbH, Metzlerstrasse 26, 60594 Frankfurt am Main.*

In Spain: Please write to *Penguin Books S. A., Bravo Murillo 19, 1° B, 28015 Madrid.*

In Italy: Please write to *Penguin Italia s.r.l., Via Benedetto Croce 2, 20094 Corsico, Milano.*

In France: Please write to *Penguin France, Le Carré Wilson, 62 rue Benjamin Baillaud, 31500 Toulouse.*

In Japan: Please write to *Penguin Books Japan Ltd, Kaneko Building, 2-3-25 Koraku, Bunkyo-Ku, Tokyo 112.*

In South Africa: Please write to *Penguin Books South Africa (Pty) Ltd, Private Bag X14, Parkview, 2122 Johannesburg.*